ALSO BY RICHARD PAUL EVANS

Finding Noel
The Sunflower
A Perfect Day
The Last Promise
The Christmas Box Miracle
The Carousel
The Looking Glass
The Locket
The Letter
Timepiece
The Christmas Box

For Children
The Dance
The Christmas Candle
The Spyglass
The Tower
The Light of Christmas

✴ RICHARD PAUL EVANS ✴

THE

Gift

SIMON & SCHUSTER

NEW YORK   LONDON   TORONTO   SYDNEY

SIMON & SCHUSTER
1230 Avenue of the Americas
New York, NY 10020

First Simon & Schuster hardcover edition October 2007

SIMON & SCHUSTER and colophon are registered trademarks
of Simon & Schuster, Inc.

For information about special discounts for bulk purchases,
please contact Simon & Schuster Special Sales at
1-800-456-6798 or business@simonandschuster.com

Designed by Davina Mock-Maniscalco

Manufactured in the United States of America

1   3   5   7   9   10   8   6   4   2

ISBN-13: 978-1-4165-5001-3
ISBN-10:   1-4165-5001-1

✧ ACKNOWLEDGMENTS ✧

irst and foremost, to my loyal readers who make everything possible.

I'd like to thank my usual partners; my agent Laurie Liss, for her long suffering, my editor Sydny Miner for her usual wisdom and encouragement, my copyeditor Gypsy da Silva for her keen eye, and my publishers David Rosenthal and Carolyn Reidy for their continued support and brilliance. Thank you to my personal assistants Miche Barbosa and Chrystal Checketts Hodges, as well as Heather McVey and Barry Evans. I am fortunate to be surrounded by such a remarkable posse.

A very special thank you to my writing assistant, Karen Roylance, for her hard work, insight, enthusiasm, and unwavering encouragement. (And picking up the Cokes at midnight.) Paul and Lynnette Cardall (PaulCardall.com), Lt. Court Williams with the Santa Barbara County Sheriff's office (Elvis has left the building), A'lynn Berg N.P., and attorney Steven Ward.

I would also like to thank my business partner, bestselling

author Robert G. Allen, and the rest of the BookWise founders: Andy Compas, Mark Hurst, Dennis Webb, and Blair Williams. Also all our BookWise Associates around the world: the most enlightened group on the planet.

And most of all, Keri. You are still my breath and my home.

✦ *To Michael* ✦

This book's protagonist, Nathan Hurst, has Tourette's syndrome and chronic tic disorder. Tourette's is an inherited neurological disorder characterized by physical and vocal tics. I also have Tourette's. The symptoms I describe in the book are based on my own.

Every good gift and every perfect gift is from above . . .

✦ JAMES 1:17 ✦

THE

Gift

*I*t's Christmas night. Everyone is asleep in the house but me. From my den window I see it has started snowing, but not in earnest. It seems to me a kind of curtain falling on the day.

There is a tranquillity to the moment that permeates my thoughts. I sit with a pencil and a pad of paper. I am prepared to write a story. This is not a Christmas story. Christmas is nearly over, dying like the fire in my fireplace, sharing the last of its warmth and light. Tomorrow the ornaments and decorations will come down, and we'll put Christmas away in boxes and bins. But first our family will visit a cemetery only a short drive from our house. I'll brush the snow from a headstone, then lay a potted poinsettia plant on its marble table. I'll hold my wife and daughter, and we'll remember a little boy.

Ours will not be the first footprints in the snow or the first flowers left. There will be two bouquets waiting. They're there every year.

You might already know some of our story—or think you

do. Some of it made the news. But what you heard was just a few bars of a song, and badly played at that. Tonight this weighs heavily on my mind. I believe it's time the world knew the whole truth, or at least as much as I can give them. So tonight, I begin to record our story for future generations. I know from the outset that many will not believe it. You may not believe it. No matter. I was there. I knew the boy and what he was capable of. And some things are true whether you want to believe them or not.

CHAPTER

One

I don't believe society has ever grown more tolerant.
It just changes targets.

✦NATHAN HURST'S JOURNAL✦

I was born with Tourette's syndrome. If you're like most people, you're not sure what Tourette's is but suspect it has something to do with shouting obscenities in public. You'd be about ten percent right.

Tourette's syndrome is a neurological disorder characterized by repetitive, involuntary movements; things that make "normal" people uncomfortable. Some of us, about ten percent, curse in public. Some of us bark or make other animal noises. I have tics. I've had more than twenty different manifestations, from vocal tics like clearing my throat and loud gulping to repeated eye blinking, shrugging, head jerking, and grimacing. My last tic was in my hands, and even though it hurt, I still preferred it to a facial tic, because you can't hide your face in your pocket.

I also have a compulsion to spit in the face of famous people. I've never actually spit in anyone's face, probably because I don't know anyone famous, but the impulse is there. I once saw Tony Danza at a Park City restaurant, and I put my hand over my mouth, just to be safe.

The most peculiar of my symptoms is my need to touch sharp objects. If you were to go through my pockets you would find dollar bills folded into sharp corners. There's linen in paper money, which gives it an especially sharp corner. But anything sharp brings me comfort. On my desk at work there are always a dozen or more highly sharpened pencils.

People sometimes ask if my tics are painful. I invite them to try this experiment: blink sixty times in one minute and see how your eyes feel. Now do that for sixteen hours straight. I remember, as a boy, holding my face at night because I couldn't stop it from moving, and it hurt.

But more painful than the physical hurts were the social ones, like sitting alone in the school cafeteria, because no one wants to sit by someone making funny noises. The panicked look on a girl's face when your own face is doing gymnastics as you ask her out. (Tics are usually exacerbated by anxiety, and if asking a girl out doesn't make you anxious, what does?) Or being surrounded by every kid at summer camp, because they want to see what *the freak* will do next. There's a reason I learned to keep to myself.

Not surprisingly, I read a lot. Books are the most tolerant of friends. There were great books back then. *Old Yeller, Andy Buckram's Tin Men, Where the Red Fern Grows, The Flying Hockey Stick.* But my greatest love was comic books. Not the kiddie rags like *Archie and Jughead,* but the Marvel ones, whose heroes had muscles on muscles, bulging through skin-tight costumes. Characters like Spiderman, Captain America, Ironman, and the Incredible Hulk. I would read my magazines before and after school and long into the night, falling asleep with the lights on. I was always dreaming of being someone special: able to walk through walls (or knock someone through one), to fly, to burst into flames, or to wrap myself in a force field—safe from whatever the bad guys could throw at me. Tellingly, the power I wanted most of all was to be invisible.

In a way I got my wish when I was eight years old. I became invisible. Not to everyone. Just to those who mattered.

✦

Tourette's wasn't the worst part of my childhood. Five weeks after my eighth birthday, on Christmas Day, a tragedy destroyed my family. Ten months later my parents filed for divorce. But it was never finalized. My father took his life on December twenty-fifth, one year to the day tragedy struck.

My mother was never well after that, physically or emotionally. She spent most of her time in bed. She never again hugged or kissed me. This was about the time my tics began.

The month I turned sixteen, I moved out. I dropped out of school, piled everything I owned in the back of a Ford Pinto, and drove to Utah to live with a former schoolmate. I never even told my mother I was leaving. There was no reason to. I was rarely home, and we never spoke when I was.

You might assume that I was the victim of whatever bad thing happened. But you'd be wrong. It was something that *I* did. I suppose that's why I don't really blame my mother for how she treated me. Or my father for taking the back door out of life. It was my fault my life was such a mess. And

Christmas was just another day on the calendar. I never believed it could be otherwise until I met Addison, Elizabeth, and Collin.

✴

The Bible says that God has chosen the weak things of the world to confound the things which are mighty. My story is about one of God's weak things. His name is Collin, a frail, beautiful little boy with a very special gift.

CHAPTER

Last night I had a peculiar dream. I was wandering at night through a desolate wilderness of dead timber and swamp. In the darkness I heard the grunts and growls of fierce things. And in the distance I heard the cry of a child, and this frightened me too. Suddenly, a woman's hand took mine. Even though it was smaller than mine and very soft, I was no longer afraid of what I could not see. There were no words in this realm, but we could fully understand each other's thoughts. "It's okay, Nathan," came the words, "I'm here." The woman's face was obscured by darkness, and I asked when I would see her. "Soon," came the reply, "When he will save you." Then she vanished. "Who will save me?" I asked in my thoughts, "Who is 'he'?" She didn't reply. As feelings of abandonment grew, I resorted to voice. "But I didn't see your face. How will I know it's you?" My words only echoed in the void. Then the peaceful, small voice returned. "You'll know my son." And then I saw him. He was bald, and my first, unchecked thought was that he looked like a Buddhist monk. His face was pale with gentle, almost feminine features. But most memorable were his piercing, clear eyes. Before he vanished, a thought came to my mind. "There's no hurt so great that love can't heal it." I wondered if that was true.

✦ NATHAN HURST'S JOURNAL ✦

NOVEMBER 15, 2002

My story began about a week before Thanksgiving. I had a fierce case of bronchitis—the kind that makes you feel like you are going to cough up your lungs. My job requires that I travel a lot, and the holidays are my busiest time of the year. So I procrastinated about seeing a doctor as I hopped around the country, downing honey-lemon cough drops by the bag.

I have an unusual job. In the age of the Internet, I am Big Brother. I work as an in-house detective for the MusicWorld chain. It's my job to keep our employees from stealing from us—or at least from getting away with it. I sit in a small, windowless office in Salt Lake City watching transactions from our 326 stores all around the country. You would be amazed at what I can deduce from my screen, watching unseen. Invisible. I know a hundred ways to steal from our stores, and every week some fool somewhere tries one of them, thinking he's the first guy to try it.

My job is like fishing. (Back at the home office, we call suspects "fish.") I troll for a while until I hook something.

Then I play with them on the line until I have enough evidence to fly out and have them arrested. The routine's pretty much always the same. I arrive, unexpected, at the store with a police officer in tow. We confront the employee and take them to a back room where we spend an emotionally charged hour or more interrogating them.

I've come across all kinds of thieves, from Goths and high school dropouts to honor students and Eagle Scouts, even a gray-haired grandma in Akron who looked like Mrs. Santa Claus.

I'm no sympathizer with thieves, but sometimes I feel bad for them for succumbing to a momentary lapse of judgment or, at least, of conscience. Oftentimes they have bigger problems, an addiction or a bad debt. Most disturbing are the sociopaths, unencumbered by conscience or guilt, just taking what they feel entitled to. These people feel no remorse—only rage at me for getting in their way. In fact, they usually blame me for their problems. In their twisted sense of reality, things were going pretty well until I showed up.

After four years of doing this, I've developed a very effective system of interrogation. I don't say much. The less the better. I let the accused in on a few details of their crimes, the ones I know about, and hint that I know more. Then I sit with a pad of paper quietly taking notes, letting them do as much talking as possible, mercifully giving them a chance to fully confess and find some leniency from us and the courts. The truth is mercy has less to do with this than practicality. I don't always catch everything they've stolen; and they don't know what I know or, more importantly, what I don't. I once had a woman confess to nearly twenty thousand dollars of theft I'd missed.

When we're done with our conversation, the police handcuff and frisk them. Then we walk them out in full view of the other employees to a waiting police car. The "walk of shame," we call it. Not surprisingly, internal theft goes way down in any store I visit. I save my company more than a million dollars a year, and that's just the merchandise we recover. Like I said, I have an unusual job.

The holiday season is not just a time for giving; it's also the worst time for employee pilfering. It was Thursday, a week before Thanksgiving, when I made a quick trip to Boston, where two temporary holiday employees, fraternity boys, were stealing guitars and having their "brothers" return them for cash. They were pocketing over three thousand dollars a day and saving the money for an "unforgettable" (their word, not mine) New Year's Eve frat party. I think they got their wish. I'm sure they'll never forget the New Year's they spent in jail. My next stop was Philadelphia.

The thief I'd apprehended was named Jenifer—one "n"—a twenty-five-year-old woman who had stolen almost six thousand dollars of merchandise.

Sitting in the back room of the store with us was a police officer, the store manager, and his assistant. The store manager was older than most I'd encountered over the years, a Woodstock throwback with his long, silver hair twisted in a Jerry Garcia ponytail. The assistant manager was much younger, in his early twenties, and as tightly wound as a violin string. He glared fiercely at the young woman, and I could imagine him in a darkened room alone with the suspect, a bright light glaring in her face as he smacked the table with a truncheon, demanding her confession.

The young woman didn't make eye contact with any of us but sat with her head down, shaking with fear.

Personally, I felt like death. I had a fever and chills, and had just come from the bathroom where a coughing spell had nearly dropped me to my knees. If I hadn't already brought in the police, I would likely have just skipped the interrogation and found an urgent care clinic instead. After ten minutes of a mostly one-way interrogation, the young woman glanced up at me and asked softly, "Can I talk to you alone?"

This was a violation of company policy, as well as common sense. Being alone with a suspect invites bribes, threats, and accusations. I had nothing to gain, everything to lose. Still, I considered. I had conducted more than two hundred interrogations, and this one felt different. Something was missing from her story. After a moment, I nodded to the other men, and, though they were clearly miffed, they left the room. When the door was shut, she looked up at me, her chin quivering, her eyes red with tears.

I brought out my Dictaphone and turned it on. "I'm recording everything you say, so I advise you to not try to bribe or threaten me."

She shook her head. "That's not why . . ."

"What do you want to say?" I asked.

"I stole."

"We've established that."

She looked back down. "I've never stolen before. I'm just trying to leave my husband." Then she brushed the hair back from her ear, exposing a large black and purple bruise. "He takes my paychecks, and I thought if I could get a little money on the side . . ." She struggled to regain her composure. "I couldn't do it. I brought everything back, but then I didn't know how to sneak it back in the store without getting caught and losing my job. Is there a way you can punish me without anyone finding out?"

"You mean your husband." I could see the terror that word evoked.

"I don't know what he'll do to me . . . and my little girls . . ."

It was then I realized that she wasn't afraid of me or the police or even jail. She was afraid of *him*.

I just looked at her, unsure of what to do. There was no doubt in my mind that she believed she was in danger. This was uncharted territory for me.

I burst out in another fit of coughing. When I recovered, the only sound was her sobbing. She covered her face with her hands.

"You brought everything back?"

"It's still in the trunk of my car."

"*Everything* is in your trunk?"

She nodded again.

After another few moments, I asked, "Where's your car?"

"It's out back. It's a white Corona."

"Give me your keys."

She surrendered a large key ring attached to a small, egg-shaped acrylic frame with a picture of two smiling little girls.

"Come on," I said.

Together, we walked out of the room and past the men on our way out to the parking lot. They curiously watched us leave, and the assistant manager walked us to the door as if anticipating our escape.

The car was a wreck. The windshield was cracked, the back panels were rusted out, and the vinyl seats inside were mostly shredded, exposing springs and foam rubber. I opened the trunk.

Everything was there, price tags and brochures still attached. I leaned against the car and coughed. "Help me carry this stuff inside," I said.

I took the amplifier, while she carried the two guitars. We returned to the back room and set everything down in the corner. Then we sat back down. She looked at me expectantly. Just then the manager returned with his assistant and the police officer. She immediately tensed up.

"So, what's up?" the assistant asked tersely, angry that he'd been asked to leave.

"I think we should let this one go," I said. "She was just borrowing everything for a party. She brought it all back. It's all there, and nothing's damaged."

The cop and the assistant looked at me as if I had lost my mind.

I turned to the store manager. "It was dumb, but she wasn't stealing. At least, that wasn't her intent. I recommend that you charge her a rental fee and put her on probation."

The assistant manager came unglued. "You believe her? Just look at her. You can tell she's lying! Send her to jail."

The manager ignored the outburst. He asked the woman, "Is that true? You were just borrowing everything?"

She didn't look at him, but nodded.

The assistant groaned. "This is the stupidest thing I've ever heard. She's a thief." He turned to me. "What did she say after we left? What did she offer you?"

I covered my mouth and coughed again, then turned my pad of paper to a blank sheet and began writing. When I was finished, I tore the sheet out and handed it to the assistant manager. He took the paper and, as he read it, his expression changed. He furtively glanced at me then stood and left the room.

I turned to the store manager. "It's your call."

As he looked at the woman, I saw in his eyes the kind of compassion that comes from being knocked around by life a time or two. "I never thought Jen did it in the first place," he said quietly. He stood, picked up the guitars by their necks and turned back to the woman. "Put the amplifier back and go to your counter. We've got a lot of work to do." He said to me, "You should see someone about that cough."

He walked out of the room. The officer looked at me. "I guess we're done." He shook his head as he stood and walked out, leaving just the two of us.

After a moment the young woman said softly, "Thank you."

"I'm going to have to report the abuse."

"I understand."

"Get away from him. Take your girls and go to a woman's shelter if you have to." I stood. "And don't steal anymore."

"Sir?"

"Yes?"

"What did you write that made him go?"

I smiled a little. "You're not the only one in this store I've had my eye on."

CHAPTER

Three

"Oh, the weather outside is frightful,
Now I'm stuck in the Denver terminal,
And they say there's no planes to go,
There is snow, too much snow, stop the snow."
(I think I'm losing my mind.)

✶.NATHAN HURST'S JOURNAL.✶

It was my birthday. Not that that meant anything more than a quick mental acknowledgment. At the end of the day I would mark it off my calendar like any other. I had a two-hour layover in Denver on my way back home to Salt Lake City. Breathing the stale, recycled air of the plane intensified my cough, and I wanted nothing more than to be home in bed or breathing in the steam of a hot shower. Unfortunately, the weather had other plans.

It had already been snowing for more than six hours, but the real front came in on our tail. From my window seat, Denver looked as white as a wedding cake.

A few moments after we landed, I turned on my cell phone. My office assistant, Miche, had left me a voice mail informing me that in the event the airport closed, she had reserved me a room in the airport hotel. She had booked the presidential suite, as it was the last room available. "I had to get it cleared from accounting," she said brightly and I detected a slight gloat. I could imagine her battle with the pencil warriors in accounting. "They said not to get used to it. I hope you're feeling a little better. I scheduled a doctor's appointment for you at the Midvalley Clinic for tomorrow. So get some rest. And by the way, happy birthday, boss."

Love that woman. I tucked the phone into my jacket pocket. Our plane docked; I grabbed my briefcase, then filed out the jetway with the rest of the passengers.

The terminal was teeming with stranded travelers. People filled the seats, overflowed onto the carpet, and spilled over onto the tile floors along the sides of the terminal like campers lining the road the night before a parade. *Thank goodness for Miche,* I thought. I passed a candy store and made a mental note to pick her up some chocolates.

Christmas music was playing, and the refrain "Let it snow, let it snow, let it snow" reverberated throughout the terminal. The corridor was bright, the windows pelted with a snowfall that showed no sign of faltering. I glanced up at the airport departure display. The word CANCELLED filled every time slot. It was clear that we were going to be here a while.

The small fast food joints weren't prepared to feed the masses, and many of them had already closed, their metal security grilles pulled down, their employees huddled inside like convicts. Even the sundry shops with their candy and nuts were picked clean of merchandise like a Florida supermarket in hurricane season. I crossed the terminal and joined a long line outside the Delta help counter.

That's where I met Addison.

She was pretty—not in a magazine cover way, but, to my way of thinking, even better. She was comfortable. She looked a few years younger than me, and almost a head shorter with long, cappuccino-colored hair that turned up on her shoulders. She had several bags draped over her shoulders and a black roller bag at her feet.

Her little girl—the only one around us who still showed signs of life—was jumping between the lines on alternating feet, playing hopscotch on an imaginary turf, when she accidentally fell into the businessman ahead of her mother. In the chaos of the moment, tempers were short and the man, finding someone on whom to vent his frustration, wheeled about, his face red, a vein bulging from his neck. He was an egg of a man, dressed in a vested, pinstriped suit.

"Watch it!" he shouted.

The woman grabbed her daughter by the shoulders and pulled her close. "I'm sorry."

Pretty much everyone in line looked to see what had provoked the outburst.

"Control your child!"

The woman flushed. "I'm really sorry. She's just been cooped up all day."

"Then leave her home if she can't behave."

That's when I noticed the boy clinging to her arm. He was small, likely eight or nine years old and he was remarkably thin and frail looking. He wore a Utah Jazz cap, but there was no hair beneath it, not even eyebrows or eyelashes. A surgeon's mask covered his nose and mouth. Letting go of his mother's hand, he clenched his fists and faced the man.

"Don't talk to my mother like that!"

The man pushed a finger at the little boy. "You watch your mouth, you runt . . ."

Something inside me snapped. Before I knew it, I had stepped toward the man. "What's the matter with you? A little girl bumps into you and you lose your mind? She said she was sorry. Now turn around and leave them alone."

There were snickers all around us, and I heard an echo of people repeating to others what I had said. The man was caught squarely between his fear of me and public humiliation. I'm six foot one, with a forty-two-inch chest. One of my hobbies is weightlifting, so I can look pretty menacing when I want. I probably looked like a madman, my face and hands twitching and sweat running down my face from my fever. The businessman was at least four inches shorter than me, and about as muscular as a strand of kelp.

Cowardice won out. He turned around, cautiously grumbling to himself.

The woman glanced furtively at me, but didn't speak. She seemed as embarrassed by my intrusion as she was by the man's outburst. She pulled her daughter into her. "No more running around," she said.

"But I'm bored."

"I know, honey. It will just be a few more minutes."

The little boy turned and looked at me, and for a moment I thought I knew him from somewhere. I turned away as another coughing spasm took over me.

It was another half hour before she reached the gate agent, a stout, surly Arabic man who impatiently took her ticket.

"I was on flight 2274 to Salt Lake," she said.

"It's been cancelled," he replied curtly.

She ignored his statement of the obvious. "Do you know when we'll be able to fly out?"

He looked at her ticket and shook his head. "You're flying standby? From the look of things, I'd say sometime next spring."

She sighed audibly.

"Mommy, I'm *hungry*," the girl said.

"When we're done, we'll find something." She turned back to the man. "Do you give out hotel vouchers?"

"Vouchers?"

"For free hotel rooms."

"That's only if the cancellation is the airline's fault, not for acts of God."

"Do you have some kind of a hotel discount?"

"No. But it wouldn't matter if we did—the roads out of the airport are closed. And it would be a miracle if there were a room left at the airport hotel. You'll just have to camp out like everyone else."

I could see the distress on her face. She gently rubbed the back of her son's head. "Thank you," she said softly. "Come on, kids."

The man turned his attention to me, extending his hand for my ticket. "Next."

I watched as the little family walked away.

"Next."

I stepped forward and handed him my ticket. "I was on that same flight to Salt Lake," I said. "I just wanted to make sure I'm rebooked on the first flight out."

He examined my pass. "You're first class and platinum medallion. You'll be taken care of."

"Where's the hotel?"

"Up near gate C23."

"Thank you."

I lifted my bag and walked back to the candy store, Rocky Mountain Chocolates. They were nearly sold out. I bought a huge box of hand-dipped chocolates for Miche. I knew she would give me obligatory grief about the size of the gift, as she'd been trying to lose five pounds for the last six months.

My coughing must have been pretty intense, because the woman at the counter put a napkin over her mouth. She also had me run my credit card through the machine myself so she wouldn't have to touch it.

I stored the candy in my briefcase, then made my way down the corridor, toward the hotel. I again saw the woman and her children. She had stacked her things against a wall, and the three of them sat on the tile floor. Her daughter's head lay in her lap and her son leaned into her. The girl was eating a strand of red licorice, her mother was knitting. The sight of them huddled together reminded me of a breathing version of Dorothy Lange's "Migrant Mother," though not so pathetic. I stopped a few yards in front of her.

"You okay?" I asked.

She looked up at me and set down her needles. She had amazingly beautiful eyes, deep and almond-shaped. "Yes. Thank you."

"I didn't mean to embarrass you. That guy was out of control."

"He was just frustrated," she said. "Just like the rest of us. But thank you."

I took a step toward her. "I'm Nate Hurst."

"I'm Addison Park."

"It's nice to meet you, Addison. This might sound a little forward, but I couldn't help overhearing you . . . I have a room reserved at the airport hotel. Actually, it's a suite, so there are two rooms. You and your children are welcome to take one of them."

I couldn't quite read her expression. I guessed she was contemplating what I would expect in return.

"Thank you. But we're okay." It was an obvious fib, told in the same tone of a child reluctantly refusing candy offered by a stranger.

"I know it doesn't help to say I'm not a weirdo or a serial killer, because that's probably what a weirdo or serial killer would say . . . but I'm not. And you've got kids. You all look pretty tired."

She brushed a strand of hair back from her face. Her voice softened. "We've been traveling for days, and my son isn't well. He's just been through chemo, and his immune system isn't strong."

I wondered what would get her on a plane with a child in this state. "And here I am coughing all over," I said. "If it makes you feel better, I'll just give you the whole suite. I can camp out in the Crown Room." A look of wonder crossed her face. I guessed she couldn't believe I'd just offered her my room. I suppose I couldn't either. "Come on," I said. "This is no place for kids. Another hour and they'll probably start eating each other."

She laughed, and in spite of her obvious distress her laughter was warm and sweet. Her expression relaxed. "Thank you. That's very kind of you."

I burst out in a fit of coughing. "Let's go. I'll get you checked in."

She gently lifted her daughter's head. "C'mon, honey. We're going to a hotel."

The little girl looked at me curiously. "Why does his eye blink like that?" she asked. "It's like a horse."

Addison blushed. "Lizzy, don't be rude."

"I have Tourette's syndrome," I said. "It makes my eye do funny things."

"Can't you stop it?"

"Sometimes. But it's like holding your breath. You can do it for awhile, but eventually you'll have to breathe."

"Does it make you cough too?" the boy asked.

"No, that would be something else."

Addison stepped close to me. "I'm so sorry."

"It's okay."

I grabbed her bag. Addison took her children's hands.

"My name is Elizabeth," the girl said. "But my mom calls me Lizzy. That's short for Elizabeth. This is my brother, Collin."

"My name is Nate. It's nice to meet you."

"Pleased to meet you, sir," Collin said.

I liked the kid. Actually, I'd liked him since the moment he stood up for his mother.

"I'm pleased to meet you too," I said, extending my hand. He didn't reciprocate.

"I'm not supposed to shake hands."

"Sorry."

"Are you married?" the little girl asked.

Addison shot her a disapproving glance.

"My daddy left. He's a crumb."

"That's enough, Elizabeth," Addison said, flushing slightly as she turned to me. "I'm so sorry. I'm afraid you're going to regret your offer. I'm sure you already do."

I just smiled.

We walked the short distance to the hotel, and I got in the long line at the registration counter. It took nearly forty-five minutes to check in. Addison was knitting again when I brought her the key to the room.

"Sorry that took so long. Let me help you with your bags."

"You don't need to. We've wasted enough of your time."

"I've got nothing but time."

We took the elevator to the seventh floor, then walked down to the end of the corridor to the suite. I opened the door, then stood back and let them enter.

"Oh, my." Addison said, as she walked into the room.

"This is bigger than our house," Elizabeth shouted, circling the room with her arms open wide.

"It's the presidential suite," I said, and was seized with a burst of coughing.

"You must be someone really important," Collin said.

"No. It was just the last room they had."

I stepped inside after them but stayed just a few feet from the door, like a porter.

Addison turned and looked at me. "You don't know how much I appreciate this. We've been almost three days trying to get home. A friend of mine works for Delta and gave us buddy passes. We keep getting bumped."

"Your friend should have known better than to let you fly standby the week of Thanksgiving."

"She warned me. I just didn't have much of a choice." Addison suddenly glanced at her watch. "Oh, no. I forgot to change my watch. Collin, you need your medicine, pronto." She unzipped the largest of her bags and brought out two plastic pill bottles. She spilled a pill from each container into the palm of her hand then filled a glass of water from the sink. She gave the glass and the pills to Collin. "There you go."

"Thank you."

"Look, candy!" Elizabeth shouted. She ran to the dining table, where there was a plate of strawberries dipped in white and dark chocolate.

"Liz, that's not yours," Addison said.

She lifted a card from the table. " 'Happy Birthday'? Whose birthday is it anyway?"

"It's my birthday," I said.

"Happy birthday," Elizabeth said.

"Thanks."

"Of all days to get stuck in an airport," Addison said.

"Just my luck." I said this more out of obligation than feeling.

"Can we have a birthday party, Mommy?"

"Thanks, but I better be going so you can get some rest."

"Wait. Please." Addison leaned over and whispered into her son's ear. The boy looked at me with an intensity that was surprising for a kid, then he looked back at his mother and nodded. The exchange struck me as rather peculiar.

"I don't feel right about kicking you out of your room. It's your birthday, and you're sick. We'll be fine here on the couch."

I was surprised that she'd changed her mind about me staying, but I was glad she had. I wasn't looking forward to sleeping on the floor in the Crown Room.

"Are you sure?"

"We'll be fine out here."

"No, you take the bedroom. That way you can all share the big bed."

"Thank you."

I brought my bag inside and closed the door. "So, have you eaten?"

"Not much. I don't think they serve meals on flights anymore."

"Yeah, that kind of went away." I walked over and lifted the room service menu. "Do you like pizza?" I asked Collin.

"Yes, sir."

"Pepperoni?"

"Yes, sir."

"Root beer? Sprite?"

"Root beer," Elizabeth said. "Collin likes root beer too." With that she ran out of the room.

I picked up the phone and dialed room service. I ordered a large pepperoni pizza, a couple of root beers, a plate of fries, and for good measure two pieces of chocolate cake. My company gave me a generous travel per diem that I rarely met. Perhaps I would tonight. I looked at Addison, covering the mouthpiece with my hand. "What would you like?"

"I can just share with the kids," she said.

"Do you always have trouble accepting things?"

She smiled. "I guess I should work on that."

"How about starting with a salad? There's Cobb, or Caesar with chicken?"

"The Caesar."

"And two Caesar salads," I said to the server. I hung up the phone, then called housekeeping to order up a couple extra pillows and a blanket.

"Do you mind if I shower?" Addison asked.

"It's your room," I said. I again erupted in coughing. This time the spasm was pretty violent. I'm surprised I didn't burst a blood vessel. When I turned back around, Addison had a sympathetic look on her face.

"I really shouldn't be around your son," I said.

"Well, it's you or a thousand sick people in the terminal," she said. "How long have you been sick?"

"About two weeks. It's bronchitis or something."

Collin suddenly crossed the room to me. He looked at me with concern. "Does it hurt?"

"Not too much. Just when I cough really hard."

"When I go to the hospital it hurts."

I looked at the little boy with the surgeon's mask and

3 2

I felt a pang of sympathy. "I think you're much braver than I am."

Just then Elizabeth bounded back into the room. "Mom, there's two TVs. We can watch two shows at the same time."

I suddenly doubled over with another bout of coughing. While my head was down, Collin touched his hand to my shoulder. It's difficult to explain what happened at that moment; it was unlike anything I'd experienced before. When he touched me, I felt a surge of energy pass through my entire body. But it was more than that, as there was something almost emotional about it—like the chills you get when you read a powerful passage in a book or listen to a stirring piece of music. Collin stepped back and looked at me, as if awaiting my reaction, then turned and walked toward the bedroom, staggering a little with each step.

I just looked at him, unsure of what had just happened. I turned to see Addison's reaction, but she was still talking with Elizabeth. She then turned and said, "I think we'll go shower now. Come on, Lizzy."

They left the room. I felt my forehead, and though it was still moist, it was cool. I took a long deep breath, something that just five minutes earlier would have been impossible to do without coughing. I sat down on the couch, my mind reeling. I had heard of such things as the gift of healing. I'd even seen the so-called faith healers on television who, with the garish theatrics of WWF wrestlers, smacked the demons of infirmity out of the faithful, then called on viewers at home to put their hands on their TVs and be healed (and to send in a hundred bucks to show their gratitude).

But what this boy had done was entirely different. If it was a faith healing, the faith was all on his part, as I didn't even know what he was going to do. But I couldn't deny that I had felt something. And my cough was gone. A few minutes later, I realized that so were my tics.

CHAPTER

Tonight I shared my hotel room with a woman and
her two children. I believe that her boy
healed me of my Tourette's. Incredibly,
my thoughts are more on the mother than the boy.

✦ NATHAN HURST'S JOURNAL ✦

For several minutes, I just sat on the couch, trying to understand what had happened. Without thinking, I did what I always did when I was vexed: I took a twenty-dollar bill out of my wallet and folded it into a triangle. After twenty years of doing this I can fold a bill into a knife-sharp corner with one hand. I first tickled my arm with the money, then ran the point around my lips.

Housekeeping came by with the blanket and pillows I'd ordered. Then the food came. I signed the bill without speaking to the server. It was another fifteen minutes before Addison came back out. She opened the door, then knocked to get my attention.

"Come in," I said.

She looked fresh. Her hair was pulled back and she had put on some makeup.

"I just washed off three days of airport," she said happily. She spotted the tray. "Oh, the food came."

Elizabeth ran into the room screaming. "Pizza! Collin, the pizza's here."

Collin followed her in. He was no longer wearing the mask. "Mom, can we watch a movie?"

"Honey, no. It costs money. Just watch TV."

"It's okay," I said, looking at Addison. "I mean, if it's okay with you."

"Can we?" Elizabeth asked, "Please?"

"Okay. But just one. Then you have to go to bed."

"Mom, can we eat on the bed?" Collin asked.

"No."

"Can we eat in front of the TV?"

"Yes."

"All right! C'mon, Lizzy."

Addison set our salads on the coffee table, then pushed the cart into the other room. She shut the door and sat down next to me, then lifted the covers off the salads. My mind wasn't on the food. I wanted to say something about the miracle I'd just experienced, but wasn't sure how to approach it without sounding crazy.

"These look good," Addison said. She handed me a fork and knife. "So, you must have children. You know how to please them."

"No. But my assistant accuses me of still being one." I retrieved my birthday plate of chocolates and set it on the coffee table beside our salads.

"May I have one?" Addison asked.

"Help yourself."

She lifted a white chocolate–dipped strawberry and took a bite. "That's delicious."

"They're from my assistant, Miche. She is the one who booked this room."

"I like her."

I walked over to the minibar. "Want something to drink?"

She started to say no, but caught herself. "I'd love something. Is there any ginger ale?"

I rooted around until I found one. "Canada Dry." I took a cranberry juice for myself. I walked back and handed her the can, along with a glass. She popped open the lid and poured it in.

"We should sing 'Happy Birthday'," Addison said.

"It's okay if we don't," I replied.

"Then at least a toast." She lifted her glass. "To your birthday. And to your generosity."

We touched glasses, then drank.

I set my glass down on the end table. "So, where are you coming from?"

"Virginia. My father just passed away."

"I'm sorry."

"Me too. He was a good man," she said sadly. "How about you? Where are you coming from?"

"Boston, then Philadelphia. It was business."

"What do you do?"

"I'm in security. I work for MusicWorld." I've learned to give the short answer. Sometimes people get uncomfortable when I tell them I have people arrested. "How about you?"

"With Collin the way he is, I need to be at home. Fortunately, I get alimony. I put my ex-husband through law school, so it's payback, I guess. Things are a little tight, but I have a little business at home." She took a bite of her salad.

"Tell me about Collin."

She sighed a little. "He has leukemia. He just finished his

last round of chemotherapy. But he's doing well; his doctor says he's in remission. We just take it one day at a time." After a moment she forced a smile, ready to change the subject. "So, where is home for you?"

"Salt Lake. The Sugarhouse area. I was booked on the same flight you were."

"Think we'll ever get home?" she asked.

"Someday. Maybe."

"Maybe," she repeated. We ate a little in silence. Then she looked at me quizzically. "You've stopped coughing."

I shrugged. "I got better."

"Just like that?"

"I think your son healed me," I said with mock facetiousness.

The smile left her face. She glanced down at her watch. "Well, it's getting late. I better let you get to bed." She put down her utensils and replaced the silver cover over the top of her plate. "Thank you again for everything."

"I'll see you in the morning."

She walked to the door.

"Hey, may I ask you something?"

She turned back. There was an anxious look on her face.

"What made you change your mind about me staying?"

"Collin said you're a good man."

I nodded even though I didn't understand. What woman relies on her nine-year-old son to evaluate men?

"What about you? What made you ask us to stay?"

"You looked kind of desperate."

"You always invite desperate women to share your room?"

"No, you're the first. But I might make it a habit. It's been kind of nice."

"It's been nice for us too. Good night."

"Good night," I said. She disappeared behind the door.

I threw the cushions off the couch and pulled out the fold-away bed. Then I turned off the light and lay back to think. Still no tics. I wondered how long it would last.

CHAPTER

Five

I finally made it home. Even with the delay my fish,
Earl, is still alive. I don't think Earl will ever die.

✦ NATHAN HURST'S JOURNAL ✦

It was still dark when I knocked lightly on the bedroom door. Addison opened it just enough to show her face. Her hair was tousled and her eyes were still heavy. She steadied herself against the doorframe. "Hi," she whispered. "Are you leaving?"

"Yeah. They're flying again. I wanted to say good-bye."

"Thank you so much for everything." She ran her hand over her forehead, pulling back her hair. "Do we need to leave now?"

"No. I called the airline. You've got seats on the one-thirty flight."

"How did you do that?"

"I told them about your son's medical condition and they found a way to get you to the top of the list. I also called the front desk and got you a late checkout, so you can stay in the room until one. Just don't miss your flight."

"I don't know how to repay you."

"It's not necessary." I reached into my coat pocket and took out a business card. "Just in case you need a deal on a guitar . . ."

She smiled. "You're very sweet. Thanks for saving us."

"You're welcome." I started to leave.

"Nathan."

I looked back.

"The world could use more men like you."

I smiled then walked away. She didn't know what kind of man I really was.

·✦·

My flight landed in Salt Lake around ten. The landscape was white but the sky was a clear blue. Once I was reunited with my luggage, I took the shuttle to long-term parking. I broomed four inches of powder off my car, then drove into work. Miche was both pleased and surprised to see me. Miche is small—five foot nothing with blonde hair and an infectious smile. She was wearing a black turtleneck with a turquoise necklace, black suede skirt, and pink cowboy boots.

"Hey, welcome back." She looked me over. "Sleep in your clothes?"

"My suitcase was held captive in the belly of a plane."

"Which is why you always take a change in your carry-on."

"Every flight for the past four years. Except this one."

"Murphy's Law," she said knowingly. She eyed the chocolates I held in my hand. "Those for anyone in particular?"

I surrendered the box. "Thanks for the hotel room. It was a real lifesaver."

"I've got your back."

"And the birthday gift."

"You're welcome."

I reached into my pocket and pulled out its contents: a ball of wadded-up credit card receipts, and a few dollar bills folded into corners. She picked out the bills and set them in a pile on her desk, then began straightening out the receipts. It had taken her six months to accept the futility of scolding me over my practice of shoving receipts into my pockets. She had even stopped sending me out with a receipt envelope. She glanced through the slips of paper, nodding at each one. She stopped at the hotel receipt. She looked over the expenditures, then took out a chocolate and poked her fingernail through the bottom of it to see what kind it was.

"I probably exceeded my food budget," I said, anticipating her question.

"Yeah," she said. "I eat a lot when I'm bored too." She glanced again at the bill. "Wow you must have been *really* bored." She put the chocolate back and selected another one.

"It wasn't just me. I had some guests."

"Guests?"

"Just a woman I met. She was stranded in the airport."

"Wasn't everyone stranded at the airport?" Her voice turned playful. "Must have been pretty. *Was* she pretty?" She punctuated her question by popping a cordial into her mouth.

"It's not like that. She had a couple of kids."

"What? You can't be pretty and have kids?"

"I meant, it wasn't a pickup."

She looked mildly disappointed. "That's too bad."

"Why is that 'too bad'?"

"Never mind," she said, pursing her lips. "Mr. Stayner wants to see you in his office."

"When?"

"The minute Nate gets here," she said, imitating Stayner's low voice.

I grinned. She did him pretty well. "One of these days he's going to be standing behind you when you do that."

"No, he won't."

"Why so sure?"

"Because *you've* got my back."

I smiled and turned to go but didn't actually walk, because Miche is one of those people who always thinks of something else to say whenever you start to leave. She didn't disappoint. "Wait. Don't forget, you have a doctor's appointment at eleven."

"I won't be needing it."

She looked at me curiously. "That's weird. You haven't coughed once."

"I'm over it."

"No one just gets over bronchitis. Yesterday you couldn't speak without coughing."

"Well, it's gone."

"I wish I had your immune system."

"Me too. Then you'd never call in sick."

"I still would. I just wouldn't be lying in bed watching

Oprah." She smiled. "One more thing. Did you change your mind about driving to Pocatello? There are still open flights."

"I'm driving. And I've got something for you to do."

"What's that?"

"See if you can find the address for an Addison Park in the phone book."

"Addison? That's a pretty name. Would that be your mystery guest?"

"None of your business." I started down the hall. "And yes," I called over my shoulder, "she *is* pretty."

Larry Stayner, MusicWorld's head of security, had an office in the southeast corner of the fifth floor. He was a tall, thin man, a triathlete until a ruptured disk ended his Ironman prospects. He always dressed nicely. He was arrogant and self-assured, in his late forties, with hair by Grecian Formula, and thick, tortoiseshell glasses. I never really had a bead on the man, though I got along with him as well as anyone in the office. Much better than the women in the office who had nicknamed him Hands. He was volatile: generous and humorous some days, vengeful and brooding on others. I always approached him like I would a stray dog. I suspected his occasional outbursts of temper might coincide with his chronic back pain, though it might also have to do with his marriage, which from what I saw seemed as excruciating as his herniated disk.

I knocked first, then opened the door. Stayner was on the phone, but waved me forward. I stepped inside, hovering a few feet from the doorway. I quickly surmised that he was talking to his wife.

"I've got to go," he said abruptly, looking at me and shaking his head. "I've got people in my office. I'll call the contractor." Pause. "I *said* I'd call the contractor." He hung up the phone, his face contorting in anguish. "That woman could nag paint off a wall." He pushed a button on his telephone. "Martsie, call Wooden and tell him the guy he sent to fix the basement shelves put a big scratch on the stairwell wall and he needs to fix it."

He turned to me. "You're back."

"Yes, sir."

"I heard you're sick."

"I'm over it."

"Good. Take a chair."

He was clearly not feeling generous and humorous today. "So, you've been in Boston and Philly. What happened out there?"

"A couple of college boys thought we'd finance their frat house's New Year's Eve party."

"I meant in Philadelphia."

"Standard stuff. What about it?"

"Hardly standard. No arrest, and the store manager said you met with the suspect alone. Is that true?"

"Yes. But . . ."

"You must have been sick. You know what position that puts the company in. Not to mention you personally."

"I recorded the interview for our protection."

"Then you went to her car and carried two Martin guitars

and a Thomson amplifier back into the store and then gave the woman a clean bill of health."

"She helped me."

"What?"

"I didn't carry the equipment by myself. She helped me."

"And you didn't arrest her."

"She wasn't a thief."

He looked at me incredulously. "So, how did the two guitars and amplifier end up in her car?"

"She borrowed them."

"Borrowed them?" His expression turned more grim. "You know what this looks like."

"She was bringing everything back. It was in her car."

"Maybe she was on the way to a pawnshop when you caught her."

"Maybe," I said.

He looked at me suspiciously. "What's really going on?"

"Her husband was beating her. She was just trying to get some money so she could get away, but she couldn't go through with it and brought everything back."

"You believed her?"

"I didn't have to. I saw the bruises." I raked my hand back through my hair and we were both quiet for a moment. "I know. I screwed up. It seemed like the right thing to do."

"It's not your job to forgive. It's your job to keep people from stealing from us. How can I trust this won't happen again?"

"You can't."

His face showed no reaction. After a moment he slowly

reclined in his chair. "I can't fire you. You're too good at what you do. I just need to know you're not going soft. Or growing a conscience on me."

"It's a little late for that."

For what seemed an eternity he sat there, brooding. At length he sighed. "All right. You can go."

I got up and walked to the door.

"Nate."

"Yes, sir?"

"Did you report the abuse?"

"Of course."

I walked back to my office. Miche had collected my receipts in a single pile, stacked a dictionary and a thesaurus on top of them, and was pressing down with what little weight she had. She looked up at me. "So, what did Hands want? Did you let a fish off the line?"

"What are you, psychic?"

"I had lunch with Martsie." She looked at me, and her lips pursed. "You know, there's something different about you, but I can't put my finger on it. Did you shave something?"

"My legs."

She laughed but continued studying me. "I'll figure it out. Do you need anything?"

"No. But, I think I'll leave work a little early. I didn't get much sleep last night."

"Your guest keep you up?"

"Indirectly."

"I don't know what that means, but here's her address." She handed me a hot pink Post-it Note with an address scrawled in black pen. "She lives in Murray." I knew the area. It was only fifteen minutes from where I lived. "And thanks for the industrial-sized box of chocolates. Not that I need it."

"Everyone needs chocolate," I said. I folded the note and put it in my pocket, then shut my door and went fishing.

CHAPTER

Six

Stayner jumped all over me about letting that woman off in Philadelphia. I wonder what he would have done had he been there. It's one thing to order an execution, it's a whole different matter to swing the axe.

✦NATHAN HURST'S JOURNAL✦

I couldn't get Addison off my mind. I wanted to see her again. I also wanted to see her son. All day long I had waited for my tics to return. I had even faked one. Nothing. As far as I could tell, the kid had performed a miracle. I took the address from my pocket and looked at it again. Then, before I could talk myself out of it, I drove to her house.

Addison lived in a small, red-bricked rambler in Murray, Utah, a small suburb in the center of the Salt Lake Valley. (The town calls itself "the Hub of Salt Lake"—not a flattering moniker, but it probably made someone feel important.)

Her home was on a seven-home cul-de-sac just five blocks west of State Street. The front yard was a little overgrown, with pyracantha bushes, partially flattened by snow, encroaching on the house. An impressive array of icicles hung from the rain gutter in front of the house. There was no car in the driveway, but the lights were on inside.

I parked my car across the street from the home. I suddenly felt a little awkward. She had given me no indication that she wanted to see me again. I knew she was divorced, but it had been a few years, and I doubted a woman like her would stay unattached for long. For all I knew, she was involved with someone. As if in answer to my fears, a pearl white Lexus coupe pulled into the driveway. A well-dressed man in a business suit stepped out. He walked up the porch and rang the doorbell. Though I was curious, I felt a little voyeuristic watching this and decided to drive off. But before I could turn the key, the door opened and I saw her. Even from a distance, she looked beautiful.

To my dismay, they seemed pretty friendly. She hugged him, then let him in. When the door shut, I started my car and drove to the gym.

Some people deal with their problems by talking them to death. In fact, some enjoy the execution so much they resurrect their problems just so they can kill them again. Not me. Whenever I feel stressed, I go to the gym; which is probably why I can bench nearly three hundred pounds.

My disappointment fueled an impressive workout. I ran on the treadmill for an hour and twenty minutes, then went down to the free weights and lifted until my muscles burned. It felt good to work out again after being sick for so long.

I usually shower at the gym, but that night I returned to my apartment still in my shorts and sweaty T-shirt. It was cold outside, and steam rose from my body as I crossed the parking lot to my apartment. I showered, then dressed in a fresh T-shirt and boxer shorts, and sat down in my front room to read.

It was a little after ten when there was a knock at my door. I opened the door just enough to look outside. Addison stood in the hallway. "Just a second," I said. "I'm not dressed." I pulled on a pair of shorts then came back and opened the door.

She held a plate of cookies covered in cellophane with a white envelope taped to the top. "Sorry it's so late. Did I get you out of bed?"

"No. I was just reading. Come in."

"Thank you." She wiped her feet on my Welcome mat then stepped inside. I shut the door behind her.

"How did you know where I live?"

"You gave me your card. I called your office, and your assistant, Miche, told me your address. I hope that's okay. She seemed eager to help."

"Yeah. I'm sure she was."

She held up the plate. "I baked you some cookies. I would have brought them over earlier, but, like I said, I was working."

I thought of the man at her door and wondered if she was lying. "Thank you." I took the plate from her and set it on the kitchen counter.

"It's not much, but I wanted to thank you for what you did for us."

"It was nothing. Can you stay for a while?"

"Sure. Thanks." She sat down across from me and looked around my apartment, a one-room flat surrounded by bookcases.

"You have a lot of books."

"I'm all about books."

"I love to read but I usually fall asleep. There aren't enough hours in the day." She glanced down at the book next to my chair. "What are you reading now?"

"Slaughterhouse-Five."

"That's the one about the air raid on Dresden?"

"Yes."

"Sounds depressing."

"It's actually pretty funny. It's amazing what a sense of irony can do for tragedy."

"I'm afraid about the only books I read these days are my children's."

I was still thinking about the man I saw at her house. "So, you were at work?"

"Yes, well, I'm a massage therapist. It's a good way to earn a little on the side and still be home with my children. You can probably still smell the oil on my hands."

I was pleased by this revelation. "So, you work at home?"

"Yes. I have a little massage room in my basement."

"And your clients come to you."

She looked at me quizzically. "Yes."

"That's good," I said.

She laughed at my reaction. "It is good. This way I can be at home. Do you like massages?"

"I've never had one."

"Never?"

"I have this thing about being touched." I felt a little dishonest saying that. At that moment, being touched by her sounded kind of nice.

There was a little silence between us, then she smiled

sweetly. I wanted to ask her about Collin, but I still couldn't think of a way to broach the subject without sounding crazy.

"I was thinking . . . ," she said. "If you don't have other plans, I'd like to invite you to spend Thanksgiving with us. It's just Collin, Lizzy, and me."

The invitation surprised me. "Thanks. Unfortunately I'm going to be out of town."

"Oh." Her face registered her disappointment. "Do you have to work?"

"I'm spending Thanksgiving with my mother."

"That's nice," she said.

I nodded, though it wasn't true.

"Do you see her often?"

"It's been a few years."

"I'm sure she'll be excited to see you."

I didn't answer. The silence turned a little awkward. After a moment she stood.

"Well, I better get back to the kids before my babysitter revolts."

"Thanks again for the cookies."

"Thanks again for all you did."

I walked her to the door and opened it. She stepped outside, then turned back. "If your plans change, my address is on the back of the card. We'll be eating around two. She hesitated. "Or, if you just want to come over sometime . . ."

"I'd like that," I said, though I'm not sure she believed me.

"Good-bye, Nathan."

"Goodnight."

She lingered a moment longer, then she stepped forward and put her arms around me. She felt warm and lovely. She stepped back. "Goodnight."

"Bye."

She walked down the hallway and turned the corner. When she was gone from sight, I went back inside. I peeled back the plastic wrap from the plate of cookies and lifted one, taking a bite. Then I returned to my book, wondering why I hadn't changed my Thanksgiving plans.

CHAPTER

Seven

I've decided to see my mother on Thanksgiving.
I still don't know why. Maybe it's the same irresistible force
that compels us to look at a car accident as we drive by.

✦ NATHAN HURST'S JOURNAL ✦

It had been more than three years since I'd seen my mother. This would only be the third time since I'd left home. I had decided to visit her about a month earlier, and I wasn't sure why. It would probably require intense psychotherapy or hypnosis to figure that one out. I looked forward to it about as much as root canal.

The three-hour drive to Pocatello afforded me ample opportunity to turn back, and when I stopped near the Utah-Idaho border for gas, I nearly did. Too much time to think about the past. Going home, for me, was always like returning to the scene of the crime.

The entire drive, I thought about Addison. I wished I were sharing Thanksgiving with her instead. What was it about this woman?

GOLDEN YEARS CONVALESCENT CENTER—the sign looked as old as its residents. I hated the name nearly as much as I hated the place. I remember, as a boy, looking out the car window as we drove by the home and seeing the old people congregated outside. Some held canes, others leaned against walkers with bright green tennis ball feet, and then there were the ones strapped into wheelchairs. There was nothing golden about it. It was nothing more than an ancient, smelly facility for old people who hadn't the means to land somewhere better. It was the best excuse I could think of for dying young.

The parking lot was deserted, and I wondered if that was normal for Thanksgiving at other rest homes. I parked in the first space that wasn't handicap restricted, then walked inside. My footsteps echoed down the long tile corridor. The smell of the place filled me with dread. I could never quite figure out what it was—Bengay, oatmeal, disinfectant, burnt toast, mothballs, diapers—a cauldron of geriatric odors.

In contrast to the smell and palpable gloom, Christmas music played gaily over the sound system like paint spread thinly over a rusted surface. I walked to the nurses' counter at the end of the corridor. A broad, sour-faced woman with three shades of red hair color and a nose ring sat talking on the phone to someone. From her demeanor—as well as what I heard from her side of the conversation—she was clearly not pleased to be working on the holiday. I couldn't blame her. I didn't want to be there, either. After a moment she said, "I gotta go. I got someone. Save me some turkey." She hung up the phone and looked up. "Can I help you?"

"I'm looking for my mother. Candace Hurst."

"Candy's in the dining room." She studied me curiously. "You're not her son, are you? You look like you could be her son."

"That's because I am."

"She said you was dead."

"Not yet," I said.

There were only a half dozen residents inside the cafeteria. My mother sat alone at a long, bare, resin table with her Thanksgiving feast laid out on a plastic tray. There was turkey breast cut in small squares next to a perfectly round scoop of mashed potatoes, the way it looks when they serve it with an ice cream scooper; both were covered with thin, brown gravy. There were some candied yams, a splash of cranberry sauce, and a square of red Jell-O with green beans suspended on it.

When I was arms' length from her, she turned and looked at me. Her face was blank. It didn't feel like years since I'd last seen her; it felt like centuries. She looked older and smaller than I remembered, as if her head was receding into her shoulders.

"Hi, Mom."

She gazed at me, a small clot of potatoes on her lip. It was at least a minute before she asked, "Who are you?"

"It's Nathan. Your son."

"Who?"

I sat down on a chair next to her. "Nate."

"Tommy?"

"I'm not Tommy. I'm Nate."

"Where have you been?"

"I moved to Utah."

"Why did you leave me, Tommy?"

"I'm not Tommy, Mom." She just gaped at me. After a minute I said, "Here, eat your dinner." I speared a piece of turkey and handed her the fork. She looked at me suspiciously, then took it, slowly lifting it to her mouth.

"So, how are they treating you?" I asked.

She slowly chewed, looking into the distance as if she were alone. I knit my fingers together.

"Do you like it here?"

Nothing.

"My Tourette's is gone," I said aloud for the first time since I'd been healed. "It's a miracle."

Still nothing.

"They've decided to forego the next presidential election and let the candidates slug it out in a cage match. Winner takes all. It's going to be on pay-per-view."

Neither of us said anything after that. After a half hour, she stopped eating altogether. Then she suddenly looked at me, squinting as if to see through the fog of her dementia. "I miss you, Tommy."

I exhaled forcefully. "All right, I'm going."

I walked quickly out of the place, angry, but relieved to be free of its smells and memories. I got in my car. For a moment I just sat in the parking lot. I turned on my CD player to drown out my thoughts, but the music had no effect.

I hated myself for going back. Why did I do this? To punish myself? To prove that it couldn't really be as bad as I remembered?

I once read a story about a Muslim man who made his pilgrimage to Mecca on his knees, crawling for hundreds of miles until his skin was raw and bleeding. Maybe it's just human nature, the desire to suffer for our mistakes. Or maybe I'm just crazy.

Einstein said that insanity is doing the same thing over and over and expecting a different result. Maybe that's me. What did I expect? Something different? What was I hoping for? Forgiveness? That's a laugh. Forgiveness for me would be like waiting for the noon bus at midnight. I put the keys in the ignition. After a moment, I started the car and looked back once more at the center. "I miss you too, Tommy."

CHAPTER

Eight

I feel like I've been handed a prize orchid.
And I can't make a weed grow.

✦ NATHAN HURST'S JOURNAL ✦

Maybe it was the pain of the visit or the barrenness of the landscape on my drive home, but I was suddenly engulfed by an aching sense of futility. Everything in my life was pitifully the same. The same visit to my mother, the same experience in a city that never changed. The same drive home to the same job. The same lonely apartment. Nothing had changed in my life for years. I turned on the radio. No, something *had* changed in my life. I'd been cured of my Tourette's. But I realized that I had lost more than my tics; I'd lost part of who I thought I was.

I had brought with me Addison's address in case I changed my mind about visiting my mother. I wished I had. I looked at the clock on my dash. It would be past five by the time I got back to Salt Lake City. It was okay, I decided. Better late than never.

✦

It was dark when I arrived at Addison's home. I parked my car in the driveway and climbed the concrete stairs to the front porch. There were pictures of Santa and reindeer rendered in crayon and taped to the narrow panels of frosted glass that flanked both sides of the front door. I could hear the sound of someone playing chopsticks on the piano. When I rang the doorbell, the music stopped and was replaced by the hysterical high-pitched barking of a dog.

A few seconds later, the door swung open. Little Elizabeth stood in the doorway. She squealed when she saw me then ran away, leaving me on the porch. "It's that man," she shouted. "He's at our house." The dog continued its hysterics.

Then I heard Addison's voice. "Be quiet, Goldie. Hush up." The dog's yapping suddenly stopped. Addison came to the door holding a small golden Pomeranian in her arms. She smiled when she saw me. "You came," she said happily. "Come in."

"I'm late," I said, though I suspect she'd already realized this.

"I'm glad you came. Sorry Lizzy left you outside."

"No worries."

Elizabeth came back into the room and stood against the far wall staring at me. Collin sat backward on the piano bench, also looking at me. He wasn't wearing his cap or face mask, and the smooth dome of his head reflected the yellow light from above.

Addison set down the dog. It sniffed my leg, then ran off. "Let me take your coat."

"Thank you." I pulled off my parka, and she took it to another room. I smiled at the children. They just stared.

"So, you didn't go to your mother's after all," Addison said, walking back into the room.

"I went. I just didn't stay as long as I had planned. She wasn't feeling too well."

"I'm sorry. I thought she lived out of town."

"She's in Pocatello."

"What is that, a four-hour drive?"

"Three and a half. I drive fast."

She smiled. "Well, we've got lots of leftovers. Let me fix you a plate. I have turkey, dressing, and Parker House rolls. How about a turkey-on-roll sandwich?"

"No, I'm fine."

"Do you always have trouble accepting things?"

I grinned. "The sandwich sounds great."

"Good. Just sit down. I'm sure the kids will entertain you."

Addison left the room and the children still just stared at me. I sat down on a comfortable sofa upholstered in denim.

"So, did you guys have a good dinner?" I asked.

Elizabeth ran out of the room. Collin nodded.

"Eat a lot?"

He nodded again. Then he got up and left the room as well. A few minutes later Addison returned with a plate and a glass.

"Here you go." I put the plate on my lap. "And I brought you some cider. But I also have soda. Coke, Sprite, and Shasta cream."

"Cider's great." I took the glass and sipped it.

She sat down next to me. "So, you scared off my children."

"I have that effect on kids."

"I usually can't shut Lizzy up when my clients come by. They're probably just not used to having a strange man around the house who's not here for a massage." She smiled. "Not that you're strange."

"Don't be quick to assume," I said.

"I'm sorry, I better see what they're up to. I'll be right back." I took another bite as I looked around the room. It was modest but bright. There were pictures of the children on the walls and on every surface. I noticed that none of them included their father. One of the photographs of Collin looked fairly recent, except that he had hair. It was the color of his mother's.

Addison returned. "They're playing Nintendo," she said. She settled on the other end of the sofa. "So, tell me about yourself. Who is Nathan Hurst?"

"Now there's a question."

"A good question?"

"I'll let you decide. The story of Nathan Hurst is a tale of squandered opportunity and lost love."

"Sounds promising. Continue."

"I was born in the thriving metropolis of Pocatello, Idaho, where the spud is king. I moved to Utah when I turned sixteen, got a job at MusicWorld that same week, and I'm still here."

She looked at me expectantly. "And?"

"And I met Tony Danza once at a restaurant. Actually, I didn't really meet him, I just saw him. He was with a lot of other people."

"That's it?"

I nodded. "Danza's a pretty famous guy."

"I mean, your life."

"Pretty much sums up my life."

"That was the worst, condensed version of a life I've ever heard. I can see I'll have to pry."

"Have at it." I took a bite of my sandwich.

"Your mother is still alive, what about your father?"

I had to finish chewing. "He died when I was nine."

She frowned. "I'm sorry. Do you have any siblings?"

"A brother."

"And does he still live in Pocatello?"

"He died. A year before my father."

She shook her head. "I just keep stepping on landmines, don't I?"

"That's my life. One big minefield. My mother is all I have left, and she's been in a nursing home since . . . forever, and she suffers from dementia. In fact, she's not really sure who I am anymore." I leaned back and sighed. "See? The short version was better."

She looked at me sympathetically. "I'm glad you came over. And I don't mean to brag, but I make the best apple pie. Would you like a slice?"

"Love one."

"Let's go in the kitchen. It's warmer in there."

I followed her. The kitchen was small, with a linoleum floor and a yellow oak table with four chairs. "Would you like that with whipped cream?"

"Sure."

Addison lifted a can of Reddi-wip, but only air came out.

She sighed. "I'm sorry, we're out of whipped cream. Elizabeth eats it from the can." She brought a piece of pie over and set it on the table with a fork. "Would you like some coffee?"

"Do you have decaf?"

"Actually, that's all I have."

"I'm in luck."

She went back to the counter and returned with two cups, then sat down across from me.

"This is good pie."

"One of my very few talents. I love to bake. And I'm addicted to the Food Channel."

"So, I've told you the sordid details of my past. How about yours?"

"I was born in Arcadia, California, which is about as close to paradise as you can get in suburbia. We lived about two miles from the Santa Anita racetrack. There's lots of ivy and palm trees. Peacocks roam the streets and sit on top of the houses. My father was an engineer. When I was twelve, he got a job offer in Virginia, so we moved there. That's where I met my ex. We got married and moved to Utah about ten years ago. I was pregnant with Collin at the time. We divorced a little more than two years ago." She sighed. "The last few years there's been a lot of loss. My mother died about a year ago and my father, twelve days ago. He died on her birthday. I don't think it was a coincidence. He never went anywhere without her."

"How long were they married?"

"Forty-one years." She smiled. "That's exactly how it should be. My dad used to say, 'The reason we've lasted so long is because I make all the big decisions and Chrystal makes all the little ones.' And then he'd always add, 'In forty years of marriage, there's never been a big decision.' " She laughed, then said in a softer voice, "After mom died, he was just a shadow of who he was. He loved her so much. He was such a good man. I was lucky to see him before he died." Her lips rose in a slight, sweet smile. "My father was a real romantic. He used to sing Andrea Bocelli songs to my mother and me. Not that he could sing, but what he lacked in voice he made up for in heart. Or maybe it was just volume. Our favorite song was 'Con te Partirò,' 'Time to Say Good-bye.' "

"The last night I had with him, we talked all through the night. He was in a lot of pain, but he tried to hide it from me. Around five in the morning, he got really quiet. I knew the time was close. Then suddenly he looked at me . . ." She paused, and her eyes welled up with tears. "You know, that look when you're never going to see someone again. We just stared at each other. Then he said, 'It's time to say good-bye.' And he was gone." She put her head down. I let the emotion of what she said wash over me. It was a few minutes before I spoke.

"You're lucky to have that."

"I know." She wiped her eyes. "You'd think that someone who came from that would do a better job of picking a soul mate. Apparently I didn't inherit that ability."

"Does the 'ex' have a name?"

"I usually call him Darth Vader. But his name is Steve."

"Elizabeth said he left. I think she also said he was a 'crumb.' "

Addison's face screwed up like she'd just tasted something awful. "I'm so embarrassed by that. I'd never say something bad about their dad in front of them. She overheard me talking on the phone."

"So, *is* he a crumb?"

"He told me on our anniversary that he was leaving me."

"I think that qualifies."

"It's worse than that. We were on this wonderful vacation in Mazatlan, having this nice dinner, and I'm feeling all romantic, when suddenly it's like, 'how's your salmon, I'm leaving you for someone else.' He couldn't understand why I didn't stay and finish dinner. He traded in two kids and a ten-year marriage for a twenty-three-year-old blonde bra model from Venice Beach."

"A bra model?"

"Oh, yeah. He dropped that on me like he thought I would be proud of him."

"So he has a few loose wires."

She smiled wryly. "You know how before you buy a house you hire someone to come check it out and write a homebuyer's report? Someone should do that for husbands. Before you get married, you should have a complete inspection to find out what's broken, if it's fixable, and how much it will cost to repair."

I laughed at this. "You're right, except most people are more interested in being married than being right. They keep their eyes half closed before marriage, and then open them after. I once told a friend that I thought she was making a mistake with the guy she was going to marry. She said,

'Well, since we're being honest with each other, you have too much baggage to ever get married, and you should change deodorants."

"Ouch."

"Yeah. I didn't say anything after that. Her marriage didn't last a year. I wanted to do the I-told-you-so thing, but there was no point in it. At least I changed deodorants."

She laughed. "You can't tell I'm still a little bitter, can you?"

"You mean, outside of the Vader thing? No, not at all."

"I'm just really angry at him right now. Collin just went through horrific chemo treatments, and Steve didn't come to see him once. I kept having to make excuses why he couldn't be there so his son didn't feel worthless." She shook her head. "How about we change the subject. Tell me about your work."

"I sit at a computer all day and hunt thieves. It's kind of like a video game, but there's no ninjas and I don't get to shoot anybody."

"How can you tell from a computer when someone's stealing?"

"There are tricks. Of course, if someone sneaks something out of the store, there's not much anyone can do. But usually they try to convert their loot into money, write exchanges, things like that. That cash till is like cheese on a mousetrap, but whenever they go for it they leave a trail."

She took a sip of her coffee. "Did you always want to be a store detective?"

"No, my goal was to be a lawyer, but I started working at

MusicWorld as I was getting my G.E.D., and I ended up in security. It pays well, and I get my own office and assistant."

"That's Miche."

I nodded. "Miche makes my life a whole lot more livable. Like reserving the hotel room in Denver."

"Yes, I like her," Addison said decidedly. She looked at my empty plate. "Would you like more?"

"No. But it was good." We sat there for a moment. After a while, I looked her in the eyes. "May I ask you something a little weird?"

She suddenly looked anxious. "I don't know. How weird?"

I found her paranoia strangely comforting. I took a deep breath. "Something happened that night in the hotel room."

"You mean, between us?"

This was getting more difficult.

"Well, that really wasn't what I was getting at . . ." Now I felt like a real idiot. "You know, it's nothing."

Addison looked down for a moment, then said, "Collin healed you."

"You knew?"

"I was pretty sure."

"How is that possible?"

She looked down at the table for a moment, then took a deep breath as if she'd resigned herself to speak. "Collin was born with tricuspid atresia. It means one of his heart valves never developed, so basically he's operating with half a heart. They had to operate on him almost immediately after he was born to put in a shunt. They gave him a forty percent chance of surviving. But Collin's a fighter, and he beat the odds. They told me that if he lived he would someday need a heart transplant, but for the time being he was okay.

"Then, a little more than a year ago, he developed endocarditis—a walnut-sized blister in his heart full of staf infection. He needed a very serious operation. I fasted and prayed, but during the surgery things still went badly." She swallowed. "Collin died on the operating table. He was gone for nearly six minutes before they resuscitated him. I didn't know about it until he was in recovery and the doctor told me. He said they didn't know if there was brain damage. There wasn't, thank goodness, but then a few days later Collin told me that when he died, he left his body."

"Did you believe him?"

"Honestly, not at first. I thought maybe he had had a dream. Then about a week later I was knitting a cap for him when he said, 'You shouldn't have thrown that other hat away, Mom. I liked it.'

"I asked, 'What other hat?' He said, 'The one you threw away at the hospital.'

"While I was in the hospital waiting room, I had started knitting Collin a stocking cap. But his operation went almost two hours longer than they told me it would. I was halfway done with it, but I was so flustered and upset waiting for news that I kept getting off stitch. Finally, I just threw the whole thing away, needles and all. I asked him how he knew about the hat. He said he was standing next to me when I threw it away.

"Then I asked him questions about other things. The waiting room was pretty crowded that day, but I remembered that there was a young Asian family sitting in one corner of the room. They had an infant who wouldn't stop crying. Collin told me there were some Chinese people with a crying baby. He couldn't have possibly known that. He even described the flowers in the waiting room."

"That's amazing."

"What's really amazing is that he described other things not of this world. He went to another place he said was really beautiful. I think it might have been heaven."

For a moment, I was speechless. "When did you find out he could heal?"

"It was a few weeks after the operation. Lizzy had picked some roses and put them in a jar without water and then forgot about them. When she finally remembered, they had already wilted, and she began crying. Collin picked the roses up and handed them to me. I literally saw the color return to them. It was the most beautiful thing I had ever seen."

"You need to tell people about this. Just imagine what Collin could do. He could change the world."

Her expression immediately hardened. "No. They can't find out."

"Why?"

"What he does comes with a cost. It makes him sick every time. I don't know if it has a permanent effect, but in his condition . . . I'm afraid it's killing him." Her eyes filled with pain. "Every morning, the first thing I wonder is how many more days I have with him. Every time he heals someone, he gets sicker. Can you imagine what would happen if people knew what he can do?" She looked deeply into my eyes. "They would take away my little boy."

After a moment I said, "Of course. I won't tell anyone."

She reached across the table and took my hand. "I know you won't. Collin told me you'd protect us."

I cocked my head. "He did?"

"One of Collin's gifts is the ability to read people's auras. He knows things about people that they don't know about themselves. He knew things about my ex."

Things were starting to make sense. "That's why you changed your mind about staying with me at the hotel."

"Collin told me you were a good man."

Her saying this had a peculiar effect on me. It made me doubt Collin's gift: if he really knew my past he'd know better.

"There's a downside to that gift as well," she went on. "No matter how hard I try to hide it, he always knows when I'm sad. And these days it seems like that's most of the time."

Just then Collin walked into the room. In light of our conversation the normality of it all struck me as surreal.

"Mom, can we have some more pie?"

"Sure." She got up and cut him a small wedge and put it on a paper plate. "How about Lizzy?"

"She just wants whipped cream."

"She ate all the whipped cream."

"I told her."

Addison cut a second piece of pie and put it on a separate plate. "When you finish, it's time to get ready for bed. And don't forget to brush."

"But Mom, we're on level seven."

"I don't care if you're on level seventy."

"There's not seventy levels on Mario. I've never made it to seven before."

"You have ten more minutes, then turn it off."

"Okay." He walked out with the pie.

She turned back at me and smiled. "It's hard being the mom, ruining their lives all the time."

"You do a good job of it. The mom part, I mean."

She sat back down and looked at me as if expecting another question.

"Does he have any other *gifts*?"

"One I'm not sure how to deal with. Sometimes he says that he sees people from the other place. I'm not very good about it. It frightens me, so I don't encourage him to talk about it. It's like, ever since he went to the other side, he has a foot in both worlds. Nothing prepares you for something like this. I'm sure someone else would handle it better."

"I doubt it."

She smiled gratefully.

"How does a little boy process all this?"

"It's normal to him. It's all he knows. He's only secretive about it because I told him to be. But every now and then he acts on his own. Like with you."

"You had no idea he was going to heal me?"

"No."

"If you had known, would you have stopped him?"

"Probably." She looked slightly ashamed.

"He's a good kid, isn't he?"

"He has the best heart of anyone I've ever known. It's ironic, since he only has half of one." As I mused over her observation, I noticed the time on the clock above her stove.

"It's getting late. I'd better go so you can get your children to bed."

She looked disappointed. "I'll get your coat." She met me at the front door. I stepped out onto the porch, and she followed me, shutting the door behind us. She stood close, and her eyes seemed almost to glow. "You have no idea how long I've wanted to tell someone about Collin. It's such a relief."

"I'm glad you trust me."

She moved closer until our bodies touched.

"What I said, about being sad a lot. Ever since we met, I haven't felt so sad."

I looked into her eyes. "Since we're sharing confessions, I haven't stopped thinking about you since the hotel." A wide smile crossed her lips. I leaned forward, and we kissed. When we parted, we continued gazing into each other's eyes, our breath freezing in the air between us. "You know, this morning was awful," I said. "But the day actually turned out really nice."

"Mine too."

"What are you doing tomorrow night?"

"I promised the kids we could see the Christmas lights downtown. Want to come?"

"Can I take you all to dinner after?"

"That would be fun. The kids love to eat out, but we rarely do. Not in the budget."

"Where's their favorite place to eat?"

"Any place with pizza, spaghetti, or arches."

"How about The Old Spaghetti Factory?"

"Ah, you'll be their hero." She tilted her head. "You already are a hero. You already saved me once." Then she moved into me and we kissed again.

"What time?" I asked.

"Huh?" she replied, still lost in the emotion.

"What time should I pick you up?"

"Oh. We should probably eat first. The kids need to be to bed before nine. Is five-thirty too early?"

"Five-thirty it is. I'll see you tomorrow."

She waited on the porch, her arms crossed against the cold, until I started the car. She waved as I pulled away from her home. I felt as if I'd just stepped into an alternate reality, the kind you usually wake up from. A beautiful, single mother who acted like I walked on water, and a little boy who might actually be able to. I wasn't sure which was more remarkable.

CHAPTER

Nine

Sometimes I think all I have ever known are McRelationships.

✦ NATHAN HURST'S JOURNAL ✦

I suppose that I couldn't figure out what Addison saw in me. I wondered if maybe the universe was paying me back for all the years I'd been denied affection—an idea that didn't set well with me, since I didn't trust the universe. It was much more likely toying with me, the way a cat toys with a mouse before finishing it off. It's not that Addison was the first girl to show interest in me. Throughout my life I pretty much always had a girlfriend. I once heard it said that everyone needs love—and if they're denied, they'll find it, or a reasonable substitute, somewhere. Abandoned by my mother, I was always on the hunt for love. Attracting relationships is a skill, and, even with my tics, I got good at it. As recently as three months earlier, I'd had a fairly serious relationship. But my relationships never lasted. It was like they came with an expiration date, like a carton of milk.

Addison was a decided change from the other women in my life. The most obvious difference was that she had children. She had a maternal quality, which is about the most powerful force in this world. I tended to attract the opposite type—girls who, like me, shied away from commitment.

But even if disposable relationships seemed to be my

modus operandi, I had grown weary of them. Addison was certainly the kind of woman you could build the right life around. I just wasn't the right kind of man.

The thought filled my heart with dread. Our relationship had barely begun, and it was already doomed.

CHAPTER

Ten

Addison took me someplace I had never hoped to see again.

✦.NATHAN HURST'S JOURNAL.✦

Collin and Elizabeth were dressed in snow clothes and sitting on the porch when I pulled into the driveway. Elizabeth ran inside when I got out of my car. Collin sat there, calmly watching me. His stocking cap fit snugly over his smooth scalp, but his parka was too big for his small frame. It rode high on his shoulders, like football pads.

"Hey, Collin. Ready for some fun?"

"Sure."

The front door swung open and Elizabeth sprung out. "Collin, we're going to The Old Spaghetti Factory."

"Cool."

Addison stepped out after her. She smiled at me. "Hi."

I met her on the bottom stair of the porch. I went to kiss her, but she turned away, giving me only a partial hug. It was a little awkward.

"How was your day?" I asked.

"It was good. Should we take my car?"

"I can drive."

"Kids, hop in back of Mr. Hurst's car."

They ran to my car. When they were busy getting inside,

she turned and kissed me. "Sorry about giving you the cheek. I don't want to freak the kids out just yet."

It was a different kind of night for me. For the first time since I was eight, I felt like part of a family. Elizabeth took my hand as we walked into the restaurant.

A few minutes after we ordered, Collin asked, "Are you married?"

Addison covered her eyes with her hand.

"Nope."

"Are you divorced?"

"No. I've never been married."

"So you don't, like, have any other kids."

"No. You two are about the only kids I know."

He sat back in his chair. "Cool."

The children ordered Italian sodas in tall glasses and were thrilled to learn that they got to keep the glasses. Addison beamed watching the fun her children were having. She was radiant, and seemed more beautiful to me each time I looked at her.

After dinner we drove downtown. The traffic was congested for several blocks before we reached Temple Square. As we neared the center of the city, the sidewalks became crowded with people moving in herds through the crosswalks.

"Look at all the people," I said, not trying to conceal my dislike of crowds.

Addison groaned. "Of course. Tonight's the night they turn the lights on. Half the city's here. How could I have forgotten that?" She turned toward the backseat. "Kids, we'll have to come back another night."

"Aw," Elizabeth said.

Collin said nothing. He had looked tired by the end of dinner, and had said very little since we left the restaurant.

"We're caught in the flow anyway," I said. "So we'll drive around the block and you can see the lights from the street." I glanced in the mirror at Collin. "How are you feeling, chief?"

"I'm okay," he said.

It took us nearly a half hour to circle the square. We got back to their home by eight. Addison gave Collin her house key. "Will you help Lizzy get ready for bed?"

"Sure." He looked at us suspiciously. "Are you going somewhere?"

"No, I'll be right in," Addison said. "And aren't you guys forgetting something?"

"Thank you, Mr. Hurst," Collin said.

"Thanks for the glasses," Elizabeth said.

"Any time."

"Now brush your teeth and get your jammies on. And check on Goldie's water. I'll be right in."

They ran up the walkway to the front door carrying their prized Old Spaghetti Factory soda glasses.

"Do you work tomorrow?" Addison asked.

"I'm flying out to Oklahoma."

So you need to be home early?"

"Not if I can help it."

"Good. Because I have a late birthday present for you. But you'll have to come inside to get it."

Once inside the house, Addison took off her coat then

took mine and laid them both on the sofa. Do you want your present now?"

"Absolutely."

"I'll be back in a minute." She cocked her head to one side before adding, "I have a couple surprises to get ready." She gated Goldie in the kitchen and made sure her children were settled in bed, then ran downstairs. It was nearly ten minutes before she returned. There was excitement in her eyes.

"Come," she said. She took my hand and led me down the steps to the unfinished basement. We stopped in front of the first door. "Okay, close your eyes."

"What's behind the door?"

"You'll see. Close your eyes or you'll ruin my surprise."

I obeyed. She took my hand and led me into the room.

"Okay, you can open them now."

When I opened my eyes, I found myself in what looked like an exotic Arabian tent. Golden sateen sheets hung in deep folds from the unfinished walls of the basement, puddling on the carpeted floor. In the corners, lanterns hung, casting soft shafts of gold and pink light that interplayed against the darker gold of the sheets. The room was warmer than the house, and I could hear the quiet buzz of a space heater through the serene, ambient sound of ocean waves crashing against a shoreline. The smell of the room was full and rich, and, in combination with the sounds and lighting, I felt like I had suddenly been transported to another realm.

Against one wall was a narrow table with several small blue bottles and a couple of larger ones. A piece of clay pottery holding a flickering candle rested beside the bottles. In the middle of the room sat the only other piece of furniture—a massage table covered in gold sheets.

"Wow," I said. "I didn't expect this. This is so . . . luxurious."

"It's my massage room," Addison smiled. "I know it's a bit garish. I decorated it this morning in your honor. I might have gone too far. It kind of looks like a bordello."

I laughed, pleased that she had gone to so much trouble for me. "I wouldn't go that far. And it smells good."

"It's ylang-ylang, sandalwood, lavender, and rosemary. The present I'd like to give you is a massage." She hesitated. "I know you said you didn't think you'd like it, but I have a hunch you might."

I wasn't sure she was right but I wasn't about to turn down her gift. "Where do we start?"

"First you get undressed. If you're okay with that. You'll be covered the whole time," she said then added wryly, "I *am* a professional."

I started to unbutton my shirt.

"I'll step out. When you're ready, just lie face first on your stomach with your face in the headrest. Then pull the cover all the way up."

After she left, I took off my clothes and laid them in a pile in the corner. Then I climbed onto the table and pulled the top sheet up to my waist, laying my face in the cushion as she had instructed. The table was firm but comfortable, and, with the music playing, I already felt more relaxed. A minute later Addison softly called, "Are you ready?"

"Yes."

I heard her step back into the room.

She put her hand on my back. "I know it's your first time, so if you don't like something, just tell me and I'll slow down, or touch you softer or harder, or just stop completely. I want you to feel comfortable telling me exactly what you like. You're in charge. Okay? For the next hour, it's all about you."

"I like that."

"I thought you might."

Addison peeled the sheet down to my lower waist. Then she poured warm oil onto my back. I closed my eyes to the sound of her rubbing her hands together at a fast, even tempo.

She placed her hands on my lower back and began to gently massage. Her strokes were rhythmic, slow, and gentle as they moved up my back, circling over the contours of my neck and shoulders before they traveled back down to begin again.

"You're very muscular," she whispered.

I could hear her breathing slow with mine. Muscle by muscle, my body calmed under her caress until I was perfectly relaxed. I'm not exaggerating when I say I was as relaxed as I'd ever been in my entire life.

Addison's hands became warmer as she changed from a gentle, open touch to a faster and more concentrated pressure. There was something nourishing in her touch, and I wondered if, perhaps, healing ran in her family. Now, besides the palms of her hands, I could feel her fingers and forearms as she pressed into my back. I began to fall asleep. I drifted in and out of consciousness several times, and only realized I was sleeping when she softly whispered, "It's time to turn over."

She lifted the sheet to shield me, but I was so relaxed I didn't care anymore. She began rubbing my chest. Then, as she moved down to my solar plexus, suddenly everything changed.

A sickening ball seemed to form in my stomach, as if my body was turning in on itself. A terrible vision flashed before my eyes, and I gasped out loud. I found myself sobbing uncontrollably. It seemed as if I were two men. The first, my rational self, was confused and embarrassed by my display, while my other self was a sobbing shell that lay shaking, wounded, and afraid. I expected Addison to move away from me, but she didn't. Instead, she moved her hand up to my shoulder, then got down on her knees in front of me, her face next to mine.

"It's okay, Nathan," she said softly. "I'm here." She stayed there beside me for several minutes, gently holding my head with one hand as the other hand moved slowly back and forth over my shoulders and neck.

When I had regained control, I turned on my side and locked eyes with Addison's. "I don't know what happened."

She moved her hand down to the center of my back, gently tickling me. "Sometimes deep emotions are released during a massage. Memories and emotions are not only stored in our minds, but also throughout our bodies. That's why people who receive donor organs sometimes report experiencing the memories of the donor. It's called cellular memory.

"Burying emotions in our cells is a mechanism our bodies use to protect us from painful experiences. But in the long run, burying feelings only makes them grow stronger—and that creates more pain and sickness in our lives. Massage can help release those emotions. Remember when you said your life was a minefield? You were more right than you knew. But it's more like your body is the minefield. Sometimes people even report having flashbacks."

I rubbed my eyes with my forearm. "What kind of flashbacks?"

"Visions of things that happened a long time ago. Sometimes things they can't consciously recall. Or have even repressed."

"That's what happened. I saw something. It was horrible."

"What did you see?"

"My brother."

CHAPTER

Eleven

The most important story we will ever write in life is our own—not with ink, but with our daily choices.

✦ NATHAN HURST'S JOURNAL ✦

I rolled back onto my stomach, hiding my face in the table's headrest. "I better go."

"I understand," she said. She took her hand from me for the first time since she'd started. "I'll leave so you can get dressed."

She walked out of the room. I felt bad for ruining her gift, but it seemed that she understood what had happened even better than I did. I quickly pulled on my clothes and went upstairs. I was still pretty shaken by the experience. Addison was holding my coat and waiting for me in the living room. I could tell she was miserable and probably wondering if she'd ever see me again. She walked me out to the porch and put her arms around me. "I'm so sorry."

"Don't worry about it," I said. "I'll call you Sunday when I get back."

I sensed her disappointment. "I hope so."

"Of course I will. I promise."

She forced a smile. Before she let go of my hand, she said softly, almost in a whisper, "Remember, there's no hurt so great that love can't heal it."

I looked at her curiously then kissed her on the cheek and

went to my car. As I pulled my car out of the driveway, I looked back to the porch, but she was already gone.

✦

I started keeping my first journal at the age of ten. It was a homework assignment in Mrs. Domgaard's fifth-grade English class. We were required, under threat of failing, to keep a daily log of our thoughts and activities for thirty days. Eighteen years later, I was still doing it. I have an entire shelf of journals. I've become a little more sophisticated since then. I now keep my journal with three different colors of ink. I write about my day—my routine and daily activities—in black. In blue, I'm more philosophical, recording my thoughts and feelings. And in red, I occasionally write down my dreams.

When I got home that night, I went through my journal looking for red ink until I found the dream of the wilderness. It was just as I thought. Incredibly, Addison had quoted the line from my dream.

CHAPTER

Twelve

I just want to get through life
without ending up as a cautionary tale.

✦ NATHAN HURST'S JOURNAL ✦

Oklahoma was nothing unusual, but tragic all the same. The man I'd caught had been a stellar MusicWorld employee for more than eight years, which is an eternity in this business. He was a twelve-time Employee of the Month. Only two months earlier, a coworker had persuaded him to "experiment" with crystal meth as a fast way to lose weight. He was addicted after his second try. I've always been put off by the "experiment" excuse. If you said you were climbing into the lion's cage at the Bronx Zoo as an *experiment*, everyone would just think you were stupid.

Darrin (that was the man's name, though I unintentionally kept calling him Sam, probably because of his handlebar moustache which reminded me of the cartoon character Yosemite Sam) immediately began stealing to supply his habit. He was an easy catch, which is surprising, since someone who had worked for MusicWorld for eight years should have known how to cover his tracks. I suspect he subconsciously wanted to be caught. That happens sometimes.

I guessed the situation within two minutes of sitting down with him. He wore sunglasses in the dim room, and he was as jittery as a poodle on caffeine. He looked like he hadn't slept in a week, and possibly hadn't.

My interrogation went reasonably fast, which I'm certain suited him in his state, at least up until the cop handcuffed him. The truth is, I just wanted to get back to my hotel and lose myself in a book or television. I couldn't get Addison or the experience from the night before out of my mind. I hoped I hadn't done irreparable damage to our young relationship.

The lobby of the hotel was dressed for Christmas, and there was a lavish corporate Christmas party going on, with beautiful people dressed in tuxedoes and gowns. I felt like a ghost wandering through them, unnoticed and unseen. Invisible. I guess I hadn't noticed how lonely I was until I had someone to fill that void. I desperately wished Addison were with me.

I ordered an appetizer from room service and ate buffalo wings with celery stalks and ranch dressing while I watched a Biography Channel special on Vincent Furnier, aka Alice Cooper. It was quarter to eleven, an hour earlier in Utah, when I couldn't stand my loneliness anymore and called Addison. Her voice was raspy, as if she'd been asleep. "Hi."

"You awake?"

She laughed at the question. "Yes."

"Sorry. How was your day?"

"It was okay. How was yours?"

"It was good. I was just thinking about you."

"That's good. What were you thinking?"

"I was thinking that when I get back I'd like to take you out on a date. A real date. Dinner and a show."

She sighed with pleasure, though it might also have been relief. "You have no idea how long it's been since someone's made me that offer."

"Then you're overdue. Can you get a babysitter?"

"Yes. I'm so glad you called. I was afraid I'd lost you."

"You won't lose me that easily."

"When do you get back?"

"Tomorrow afternoon. I'll pick you up around six?"

"I'll be ready. Goodnight."

I lay back in bed, pleased with myself. I felt good again.

* * *

My flight touched down at three and I drove to the gym for a quick workout, then got ready for our date. I picked Addison up at six. I never met the babysitter, as she was playing Nintendo with Collin and Elizabeth. Addison practically pushed me out the front door while her children were distracted. "Trust me," she said. "It's better this way."

I took her to dinner at a cozy little restaurant called The Five Alls. The ambience is a bit like an old English pub, with dark stained beams and columns, stucco walls, and ornamental iron work. There were candles at the tables and classical music played in the background. The table was set with thick goblets and china on pewter chargers.

"I'm not dressed up enough," Addison said. "You should have told me we were going someplace nice."

"You don't have to be all dressed up to come here. Look at that guy over there. He's in jeans."

She saw the man but it didn't help because he was, I guess, a man. Fortunately the waitress came and took our orders and Addison seemed to forget her state of underdress. She ordered the chicken Kiev. I ordered the filet Oscar.

"You don't have to order the cheapest thing on the menu," I said.

"Was it?" she said convincingly. "You know, I've driven past this place a million times and never even knew it was here. It's very quaint."

"It's the best kept secret in Salt Lake. It's been here for, like, forty years, but you'd never find it if someone didn't tell you about it."

"How did you find it?"

"My first year in Utah I dated this girl who was still in high school. We came here with a group of her friends."

"Why is it called The Five Alls?"

"It's an old English saying." I pointed to the far wall. "See the stained glass window boxes? The first is the soldier. It reads, *I fight for all.* The second is the preacher. It reads, *I pray for all.* The third is the lawyer. It reads, *I plead for all.* The fourth is the king. It reads, *I rule all.* The big window over there is the taxpayer. It reads, *I pay for all.*"

She smiled. "Nice."

Dinner was a five-course meal that began with miniature sourdough breadsticks with homemade sour cream clam dip and concluded with crème de menthe parfaits.

Afterward we went to the movies. During the previews, Addison shut off her cell phone with an almost ceremonial display. She leaned over to me as she stowed it in her purse.

"You don't know how good it feels to do that. A mother needs to sever the umbilical cord now and then."

"If I were to disappear, no one would notice," I said. "Except my boss. And it would take him a few days."

"I'd notice."

I put my arm around her. The movie was a romantic comedy, not my usual fare, but it was pretty funny and it made Addison laugh, which, in retrospect, was more amusing than the show. She has a unique laugh, kind of a quick, suppressed burst like when you find something funny at church or a funeral and try to stop yourself from laughing.

We held hands as we walked out of the theater. Halfway to the car, she burst out laughing again.

"Still thinking about the show?"

"No. I was just thinking how happy I am."

I opened the car door for her. After I got in and started the car, she said, "Thank you. You have no idea how long it's been since someone made me feel this happy. Or this beautiful."

"What are you talking about? Every time I'm with you, the guys are checking you out."

"No they're not."

"You didn't see that guy staring at you in the restaurant lobby? I'm surprised his wife didn't smack him."

"I kind of noticed." She laughed. "You make me feel like a princess."

That's because you're the most amazing woman I've ever met."

She looked almost surprised, then shyly looked away. "Thank you." Her voice grew softer. "I need to apologize again for the other night. You told me you didn't like massages, and I did it anyway, and you felt obligated."

"You don't have to keep apologizing. Neither of us knew that would happen. And I was loving it up until . . ." I didn't need to finish.

Addison was silent for a few moments. Then she fished her cell phone out of her purse. "Any bets on how many times Elizabeth called?" She turned on the phone. Her expression quickly changed. "Oh, no."

"What's wrong?"

She pushed a button and the phone speed dialed. "Laurie's been calling." She turned away. "Hello."

I could hear a voice speaking quickly on the other end. Addison's demeanor changed completely. "Which one? I'll be right there." She turned back to me, her face pale. "Do you know where Cottonwood Hospital is?"

❉

I sped to the hospital. I let Addison off at the emergency entrance, then went and parked the car. By the time I walked through the hospital doors, she was gone.

CHAPTER

Thirteen

Life can change on a dime though I wouldn't give a nickel for most changes I've experienced.

✦NATHAN HURST'S JOURNAL✦

It was around midnight when a stout, redheaded woman emerged from the swinging doors of the emergency room. Her eyes panned the reception area, and settled on me. "Nathan?"

"Yes?"

"I'm Laurie, Addison's babysitter."

"How's Collin?"

"He's better now. Addison wanted me to tell you she'll be out in a little bit. But if you need to go, she understands. She's going to spend the night here."

"What happened?"

"Collin had an allergic reaction to some medication. He had a seizure."

"How bad was it?"

"Bad. The paramedics had to resuscitate him. It was close. Really close." She shook her head. "I need to go. I've got work in the morning."

I waited in the emergency room lobby for almost another hour before Addison came out. She looked very different from the woman who had been giggling and flirting with me earlier that evening. "How is he?"

"He's stable."

"What happened?"

"He started a new medication this morning. It's something he's been taking, but he'd never taken it in pill form before. It put him into anaphylactic shock." Her eyes filled with tears, but they were steady. "He almost died. He almost died, and I wasn't there. I shouldn't have left him tonight."

"You can't always be there."

"Yes, I can." She just shook her head, consumed by guilt. "I'm sorry, Nathan. But I shouldn't be doing this right now. Not when he needs me."

"You shouldn't be doing what?"

She looked in my eyes and I didn't like her expression. "You've been so good to me and my kids. But right now just isn't the best time for me to start something."

I couldn't believe what I was hearing. My chest felt heavy with abandonment—something you'd think I'd be used to by now. "Addison, you've just been through a horrible scare. But there's nothing wrong with having a friend to lean on. I can help you."

She wiped her eyes but kept a small distance between us. "I don't want to hurt you. You understand, don't you?"

"I'm not asking anything of you . . . let me help you." She just stood there and cried. After a few more minutes, she said, "I should get back. I'm sorry, Nathan."

She kissed me, then turned and walked back through the swinging doors. I stood there, stunned. We had gone from sixty to zero in thirty seconds. She had just ended the best thing in my life. I was probably standing there another minute before I walked out to my car. I don't know why I was surprised. It was what I expected. Another carton of milk.

✦

Elizabeth lay on a thin-mattressed cot next to Collin, her head propped up on a pillow. When he opened his eyes, he saw her there looking up at him. "Hi," he said.

"Mommy says we get to sleep here."

She got up and went to his bed, holding onto the aluminum side rails, her face almost fitting between them. Collin thought she looked like a prisoner in an old west jail. He could see she had been crying. He hated it when girls cried. "What's the matter?"

"They said you almost died."

"Oh, that." For a moment he didn't say anything. Elizabeth climbed up into his bed and lay down next to him.

"Are you going to die?"

"Everyone dies sometime."

"Uh, uh. Mommy doesn't die."

He looked into her frightened face. "Well, everyone but Mommy."

She wiped her eyes. "Will I get cancer too? I don't want to die."

"Nah. You won't get it."

"But what if I catch it like you did?"

"Cancer's not contagious."

"What's *con-tay-just?*

"It means something you get from someone else."

"Like you get warts from a frog?"

"Yeah. Something like that."

"Oh," she said. She scratched her elbow. "But what if I get it anyway?"

"Then I'll touch you, and you'll get better."

That satisfied her, and she moved closer to her brother. Suddenly her face brightened with a new idea. She leaned forward on her elbows. "I know. Why don't you just touch yourself. Then you'll be all better!"

Collin frowned. "It doesn't work like that."

"How come?"

"I don't know. It just doesn't."

She lay back down, and the sadness returned.

Collin pulled her in close and kissed her forehead. "Don't worry about it. You know, when people die it's not forever. You go for a while, but then you get together again. It's like when Mom and Dad went to Mexico. They came back."

"Daddy didn't."

"Well, that's different."

She thought about it. "Are you *sure* people come back?"

"I've seen Grandpa."

"You've seen Grandpa?"

"I saw him tonight."

"Why didn't I see him?"

"You just don't know how."

"What did he say?"

Collin looked at her for a while then rubbed her head. "He said, 'Tell Lizzy not to cry so much.' "

She leaned into him. "I'm glad you're my brother."

He hugged her closer. "Me too."

CHAPTER

Fourteen

I struggled to get out of bed this morning.
I think I had an emotional hangover.

✦ NATHAN HURST'S JOURNAL ✦

I suppose I lied to Addison when I said I didn't want anything from her. Of course I did. I wanted *her*. It wasn't until she turned me away that I realized just how deeply I had fallen.

I slept in the next day. I was about to call in sick when Miche called to remind me that I was meeting her for lunch. I had forgotten our anniversary.

It had been exactly three years since Miche came to work as my assistant. At the time she was just two weeks into her marriage to an accountant named Dane, a coupling I would never have predicted. Dane was a dour, humorless man who wore crisp, starched shirts, George Will bow ties, and Gold Toe socks to bed. (So I'm told.) Miche was the yang of the relationship: a free spirit. A party always waiting to happen.

She was also the perfect assistant for me. She was full of contradictions: hardworking yet playful, sardonic yet serious, childish yet maternal. She was brutally honest, as if it had never occurred to her to be otherwise. Most importantly, she truly cared about me. Having never had this kind of a relationship with a woman before, it was remarkably satisfying. She meant it when she said she had my back. Securing the hotel room in Denver was one act in a thousand that demonstrated that she really did.

I know it's probably pretty pathetic if your closest relationship in the world is with your secretary, but, as I said before, you take love where you can get it. My biggest fear was that she would someday quit to start a family, something she casually talked about. It filled me with pain every time she brought it up.

✦

For the last three years we had celebrated our anniversary in the same place: the Golden Phoenix, a little Chinese restaurant on State Street around Eleventh South. Best potstickers this side of the Pacific. Miche had taken the morning off for a doctor's appointment and she met me at the restaurant. After I ordered my traditional kung pao shrimp, the waitress took our menus and left us alone.

"Three years," I said. "I can't believe I haven't scared you off."

"You're a pussy cat. You just act scary."

"So, you're on to me."

"I had your number the day I met you." In spite of the playful banter, I could tell something was bothering her. I didn't ask. I knew her well enough to know it would eventually bubble up to the surface.

"So, you've changed your mind about going to Phoenix," she said.

"Yeah, I'm thinking the fish in store 248 might make for open sea before Christmas. Besides, I've got to get out of this inversion. You shouldn't breathe air you can see."

"Maybe Addison would go with you," she said hopefully.

"She could never leave the kids."

"You should at least ask. You shouldn't just assume—"

I didn't let her finish. "We're not seeing each other any more."

"What?"

"Yeah. We ended it last night."

"I'm so sorry, boss," she said, and was silent for a moment. "You know I pretty much stay out of your personal life . . ."

"You're all about my personal life."

"Whatever," she said quickly. "The thing is, I think you're making a big mistake. Like land-war-in-Asia big."

"It wasn't my idea to end it."

"Oh. What happened?"

"Her son was rushed to the hospital last night: he almost died. He has leukemia *and* a heart condition. She just feels like she needs to be there for him right now."

"So, who's there for *her*?"

"That's what I asked her."

The waitress returned with a platter of potstickers. Miche mixed red hot pepper oil in with my soy sauce, then pushed the small dish toward me. She was always taking care of me. I lifted a dumpling with my chopsticks. "Maybe I should have you talk to her."

"Just give me the word."

I dipped a potsticker in the sauce. "So, what did you see the doctor for?"

"Just girl stuff."

I could see the pain in her eyes. "What's wrong?"

"It's nothing."

"Come on, Miche."

Her look of pain deepened.

"You know how I keep threatening to have a baby? Dane and I have been trying to get pregnant for more than a year now."

This was a bombshell, but I didn't react, as there was clearly more to the story. Her eyes suddenly filled, and I knew how hard this was for her to discuss with me. She quickly brushed back the tears from her eyes. "The doctor says I may never have children."

Miche wanted to be a mother more than anyone I knew. I reached across the table and put my hand on hers. "I'm sorry."

She didn't say anything, but continued to look away, fighting her emotions.

"Is there anything they can do?"

Miche shook her head. "It's complicated. But even if I miraculously got pregnant, there's a good chance I'd lose the baby."

"I'm sorry," I said again.

The waitress returned with our food and set the platters down. "Anything else?"

"No. Thank you. Just bring me the check when you get a chance."

"Okay."

"I wasn't going to say anything," Miche said after the waitress left. "Now I've ruined our lunch."

"I'm glad you told me."

"I still have you . . . and you're kind of like my child."

I smiled at her.

"And I'm sorry about Addison. She's really missing out."

"Thank you." I sighed. "So it goes."

After a moment, Miche also sighed. "So it goes."

✦

I just couldn't get Addison off my mind. As much as I wanted to call her, I didn't. I just hoped she'd change her mind soon. In the meantime, I was glad to be in Phoenix. It was warm and clear, a welcome change from the cold, gray Utah weather.

MusicWorld has two stores in the greater Phoenix area: Mesa and Tempe. I had an employee in Tempe arrested. He was a journalism student at ASU and on the University newspaper staff. He kept saying, "But I have a deadline tomorrow."

"Yeah, but think of the story you'll have to write," I told him.

CHAPTER

Fifteen

It seems that the most significant events in our lives happen while we're worried about something else happening.

Mornings were always a battle. Addison put a load of whites in the washer and then walked out to the kitchen to check on Elizabeth. Just as she expected, the bowl of Cheerios sat abandoned at the kitchen table. "Lizzy, come back in here and finish your breakfast before it gets soggy. We need to leave for the bus stop in ten minutes."

Elizabeth's voice came from the front room. "Goldie got out."

Addison groaned. "How'd she get out?"

"Someone left the door open."

Addison rolled her eyes. *Someone?* "Get her, please. And hurry. We're going to be late."

"I will, Mommy." Elizabeth opened the front door and stepped out onto the porch. She cupped her hands around her mouth and yelled, her breaths clouding in the frigid air. "C'mon, Goldie. Come home. C'mon, girl."

Collin walked into the kitchen. "Hi, Mom."

"Good morning, honey. How are you feeling?"

"Okay."

"I'll pour your Cheerios. Would you check on your sister? She went out front to get Goldie."

"Okay."

Collin walked out to the porch where Elizabeth stood. "Where's Goldie?"

"She won't come. She's playing at Marcia's."

"C'mon, Goldie," Collin called, "c'mon, girl."

A puff of honey-colored fur appeared across the street, bounding through the six-inch snow, nearly disappearing between leaps.

Elizabeth started shouting. "C'mon, Goldie." She stepped off the porch and walked toward the street. "C'mon, girl. It's time for school. Mommy's going to get mad."

The dog's head rose above the snow, her snout white with powder. When she saw Elizabeth, she darted out into the street, toward the little girl.

There was a loud screech of brakes and the sound of tires skidding across pavement and ice. A gold Mercedes slid sideways as it veered to miss the dog. At first Goldie seemed to be running with the car, but the wheels caught her torso, and she tumbled and flopped beneath them.

Elizabeth screamed and ran for her dog.

"Don't run in the street," Collin shouted.

Goldie's body jerked erratically. Elizabeth crouched next to her and picked her up. "Goldie!"

The dog was still.

"Goldie," Elizabeth moaned. "Goldie."

Collin ran to Elizabeth's side, and the two children huddled around the motionless animal. "She's dead!" Elizabeth screamed.

A woman got out of the driver's side of the Mercedes and

walked back to the children, stopping a few yards from them.

Elizabeth looked up at her. "You killed Goldie."

"I'm sorry," the woman said. "She just ran into the road . . . I couldn't stop."

Addison had run outside when she heard the screech. She froze on the porch as she took in the scene: a car plowed sideways into a snow bank, her children standing close together in the middle of the road. Then she saw the small pile of fur in Elizabeth's arms and understood. *No*, she thought. *What else does she have to lose?*

Elizabeth turned to her brother. "Touch her, Collin. You can make Goldie better."

"Mom said . . ."

She looked at her brother, her faced streaked with tears. "Please, Collin. Please, help her."

"Okay." Collin leaned over and put his hand on the crown of the dog's head, then closed his eyes. The woman watched curiously. Addison walked to the edge of the road and stopped, suddenly aware of what was happening. "Collin . . ."

Suddenly the dog's hind leg jerked. Then she pushed herself up in Elizabeth's arms, licking her face.

"Goldie!" Elizabeth yelled happily, "You're alive again." She pulled her in close. "I love you, Goldie. Don't ever do that again." She turned to her brother. "Thank you, Collin."

The woman just stared at Collin. "What did you do?"

Collin looked at her anxiously and didn't answer.

"My brother can make things better," Elizabeth said.

"Elizabeth!" Addison shouted.

Carrying the dog in her arms, Elizabeth ran back to the house. The woman turned toward Addison, her eyes wide in wonder. "Did you see that?"

Addison wouldn't meet her eyes. "Thank goodness you missed the dog." She put her arm around her son's shoulders. Come on, Collin. Lizzy missed her bus, and I've got to drive her to school."

CHAPTER

Sixteen

Regret is the most tiresome of companions.

✦ NATHAN HURST'S JOURNAL ✦

Addison had just sat the kids down to dinner when the door-bell rang. Addison got up and answered it. Standing on her porch was a nicely dressed woman wearing a blue suede coat. Addison thought she looked familiar but couldn't remember where she had seen her.

"May I help you?" Addison asked.

The woman suddenly looked nervous, as if she'd just walked on a stage and forgotten her lines. "I . . ." she paused then started again. "My name is Monica Pyranovich. I was driving the car that hit your dog this morning. I know the experience had to have been a bit traumatic for your daughter, so I brought her a little gift." She handed Addison a shoe-box-sized package adorned with silk flowers. "It's a tea set."

Addison took the gift. "Thank you. But it wasn't necessary. Fortunately you missed Goldie and everyone's okay. But this is very thoughtful of you."

The woman shifted a little on her feet. "I wanted to talk to you about that. What your son did . . ."

Addison looked at her innocently. "My son?"

"Your son healed that dog."

Addison did her best to act incredulous. "What?"

"I saw your son heal the dog."

"You think my son brought her back from the dead?"

"I don't know what he did, or how he did it, but I know that dog was dead. I saw it. Why did your daughter plead with your son to touch the dog? She begged him to touch the dog and fix her."

"You know how kids' imaginations are."

"She said that your son can make things better."

Addison stepped back from the woman. "Thank you for the gift. I really need to go. We just sat down to dinner." Addison began to shut the door.

The woman put her hand out to stop it. "Please. I know I'm acting like a crazy woman. But my son is dying . . . He has a brain tumor. He doesn't have much more time."

Addison hesitated. "I really have to go."

The woman's eyes filled with tears. "Won't you please help me?"

"I wish there was something we could do."

"Do you know what it's like to watch your only son disappear a little bit more every day?"

The question pierced her. "Yes. I do."

"Wouldn't you do everything you could to save him?"

"That's what I'm doing."

Monica reached into her purse. "I'll pay you anything you ask. My husband's a doctor. We have money. I'll give you whatever you want. We'll pay off your house . . ."

"I don't want your money."

"Please. We've tried everything." She started to cry. She pushed her wallet at Addison. "Take it. Please. I'll beg, if you want. I'll get down on my knees and beg." She started to get down on her knees. "He's my only child."

Addison took the woman's arm, stopping her. "Please don't do that."

The other mother's eyes were dark and desperate; Addison knew too well how she felt. "Please, if your son can heal, have mercy on us."

For what seemed like several minutes, Addison just looked at her. The woman's pain and fear were too familiar—they were too much her own. Finally Addison said, "Where do you live?"

"We live up on the east bench, near 6200 South. I'll give you my card."

"I'm not making any promises. It's up to Collin. I won't make him."

The woman took Addison's hand and held it to her cheek. "God bless you. Thank you. Thank you so much."

"Don't thank me yet. It's up to my son."

"Of course."

"And *if* he decides to help, you have to promise not to tell anyone. Do you understand?"

"What about my husband?"

"Not even your husband."

"You have my word. No one will know." She rooted around in her purse until she found a card and handed it to Addison. "I hope we'll see you later."

"I'm not making any promises."

"God bless you."

Addison shut the door. *What have I done?* she thought.

When she had composed herself, she went back into the kitchen. Collin sat at the table alone, eating a piece of bread with butter and honey and reading the label on the honey bear bottle.

"Where's Lizzy?"

"She's watching TV. She said she was done eating."

Addison set the present on the table and sat back down.

"What's that, Mom?"

"It's a gift for Elizabeth. It's from the lady who hit Goldie this morning." Addison lifted her spoon then set it back down and looked at Collin. "Her son has cancer."

"Like me."

"It's a different kind, but yes, like you." Addison looked at him thoughtfully. "She saw you heal Goldie."

Collin frowned. "I'm sorry."

"No, honey. Never apologize for that. I'm just worried about you. She wants you to heal her son." She hesitated. "Do you want to?"

"You said I shouldn't."

"I know. But what do you want to do?"

Collin thought about it for a moment, then said, "If it was me, I would hope someone would heal me."

Addison put her hand over her eyes to hide her tears.

"I'm sorry, Mom. Did I say the wrong thing?"

"No, honey, you didn't." She reached over and put her hand on his.

"Where is the boy?"

"He's at his home."

"Are we going there tonight?"

"If you want to."

"Okay."

When the dishes were done, Addison told the kids to put on their coats and get in the car. Lizzy was already playing with her new tea set and wanted to know where they were going.

"We're taking Collin to meet a boy."

"What boy?"

"A boy like himself."

"You mean he can make people better too?"

"No, honey. He's just sick."

⁜

The Pyranovich house was in a wealthy gated community a mile west of the foothills of the Wasatch range, scarcely twenty minutes from Addison's home. She hated herself for putting her son in harm's way and more so, each mile, for not turning back. She wished that Collin had said No, but even more that she'd never given him the choice. She stopped outside the elaborate wrought-iron gate, then pushed the button on the voice box. A woman's curt voice answered. "Who's there?"

"It's Addison Park."

The voice smoothed. "I'll open the gate. We're the third house on the left."

There was a click and a whir, and the gates began to swing inward. Addison drove in, parking her car in front of a large villa-style home. Flickering gas lamps illuminated the front of the house. Addison put the car in park and took her keys.

"You kids stay here for just a minute. I'll make sure it's the right place."

A stone pathway led to the oversized glass-and-metal door beneath a large portico. Monica met Addison at the door. "Thank you so much for coming." She looked around, anxious to see Addison was alone. "Did he come?"

"I'm just making sure that no one else is here."

"It's just me and Tyler. My husband's at the hospital. I promise, no one will find out." As she said the words, Addison realized how absurd her request was. How would no one find out? Her husband, the neighbors, friends, the oncologist—how could they not notice Tyler's miraculous recovery? She pushed the thought aside. They were past that now. Besides, Addison didn't care if they knew the *what* as long as they didn't find out the *who*.

Addison walked back to the car. Collin sat in the back seat following her with his eyes. She opened the door. "You sure about this?"

"Yeah."

"Sure about what, Mommy?" Elizabeth asked.

"Nothing you need to know. Let's go in."

Both children climbed out of the car. Addison held Elizabeth's hand as they walked up to the front door.

"This is a big home, Mom," Elizabeth said. "Is this where the president lives?"

"No, honey. The president doesn't live in Utah."

The woman stared at Collin as he walked up the pathway. Her gaze made him feel uncomfortable.

"Come in," Monica said, waving them in. "Please make yourselves at home."

"Should we take our shoes off?" Addison asked.

"That's not necessary."

They had stomped the snow from their feet, then stepped inside the grand foyer. The oval room had a marble floor, and a circular staircase wound up to the second floor. Above them hung a massive crystal chandelier.

"You must have a big family," Elizabeth said to the woman.

"Why do you say that, dear?"

"Because your home could fit a million people."

The woman smiled.

"Remember what you were going to say," Addison prompted.

Elizabeth looked at her mother blankly then suddenly remembered. "Oh yeah." She turned to Monica. "Thank you for the tea set."

"You're welcome, dear."

Monica shut and locked the door. "Tyler's just down the hall. We made the library his bedroom when he couldn't climb stairs anymore."

"Does he know we're coming?" Addison asked.

"No. I didn't tell him. Just in case you decided not to come."

"Is there someplace my daughter can wait?"

"Of course. She can watch television in the family room." She looked at Elizabeth. "Would you like to watch television?"

"Yes, ma'am."

"Come this way, please." She led Elizabeth and Addison to

a beautiful high-ceilinged room with a flat screen plasma television mounted above the fireplace mantel. A black and white shih tzu was curled up on one end of the sofa.

"You have a dog," Elizabeth said, keeping some distance from it.

"That's Max. You can pet him. He's nice."

Elizabeth sat down next to the small dog and began stroking him. He looked up and sniffed her.

"He probably smells your dog," Monica said.

"Our dog got hit by a car," Elizabeth said.

Monica glanced at Addison. "Yes. I know. Would you like to watch cartoons?"

"Yes, ma'am."

Monica turned the television on by remote and began flashing through channels until Elizabeth shouted, "Sponge Bob!"

She flipped back to the cartoon. "There you are—Sponge Bob. Would you like some ice cream?"

"Yes, please."

"With chocolate syrup?"

"Yes, please. Can Collin have some too?"

"Of course he can. He can have whatever he wants."

"I like it here," Elizabeth said to her mother.

Monica opened the refrigerator. "We have chocolate chip cookie dough and burnt almond fudge."

"Cookie dough! Cookie dough is me and Collin's favorite."

She scooped the ice cream into a bowl, covering it lavishly with chocolate sauce, then brought it to Elizabeth.

"Will you be okay alone for a few minutes?" Addison asked.

"Uh-huh."

"Don't spill. And don't give any to the dog. We'll be right back."

Addison followed the woman back out to the foyer where Collin stood, his hands deep in his pockets. He was looking up at the chandelier. "Well, are we ready?" Monica asked.

"Yes, ma'am."

"My son's down here." She led them to the end of a long wood-paneled corridor lined with oil paintings. The woman slowly opened the door, then stepped inside. "Hey, Ty. It's Mom."

Addison had her hands on Collin's shoulders, and they walked in behind Monica. The room was dim, lit only by a desk lamp; the walls were lined with rows of leather-bound volumes. A hospital bed stood in the center of the room; the round, wooden table next to it was crowded with medicine bottles. Monica's son was a teenager, maybe eighteen or older, though his exact age was hard to tell with the effects of the cancer so pronounced. His head was bald and swollen from steroids, and a large scar ran from ear to ear. His breathing was shallow and labored. Monica walked over and kissed her son on his forehead. "Ty, there's someone here to see you."

Collin walked past Addison to the side of the bed. Monica stepped back. The boys looked at each other. Tyler's head was deep in a pillow, and he could only manage to turn it slightly.

"Hey," the voice came weakly.

"Hi." Collin stared at the scar on his head.

"Pretty gross . . . huh?"

Collin didn't answer.

Tyler licked his lips. "What's . . . your name?" he asked, each word a struggle.

"It's Collin."

"Where's . . . your . . . hair . . . Collin?"

"I lost it. Like you."

"Yeah . . . kinda . . . sucks." He paused. "I guess . . . I won't . . . be needing . . . it . . . anymore anyway."

Monica turned away, covering her face with her hands.

"I . . . look like . . . Franken . . . stein."

"You don't look so bad," Collin said, then turned back to the women.

"What, honey?" Addison asked softly.

His gaze traveled to Monica, then back to her, and Addison understood. "You want us to leave?"

He nodded.

"Whatever you need," Monica said, and she followed Addison out of the room.

When the door shut Tyler licked his lips. "So, why'd they . . . bring ya . . . sport? Don't . . . seem like . . . such a . . . hot idea . . ."

Collin walked up and touched his finger to the scar. Tyler just looked at him quizzically, then, as the wave of energy moved through him, he closed his eyes and breathed deeply. Collin's knees began wobbling and he collapsed to the ground. At the sound of the crash, Addison ran inside and saw Collin lying prostrate by the bed.

"Collin!" She fell to the floor, gathering her son up in her arms. "Collin, I'm so sorry, honey.' "

The woman also knelt down. "What happened? Are you okay?"

Then Tyler spoke. "Mom?"

"Tyler?"

His eyes were already brighter. He lifted his head from the pillow and looked around the room as if he'd just suddenly woken. "How long have I been here?"

"How do you feel?" Monica asked, her voice trembling.

Tyler looked at his mother. "Is this a dream?"

"No, Ty. This is really happening." His mother threw her arms around him and wept.

Tyler turned and looked at Addison and Collin, who were huddled together on the floor. Collin was conscious but lay limply in his mother's arms.

"It was the little boy, wasn't it? He did this."

Addison had pulled Collin's head into her breast and was stroking his head.

"When he touched me, I saw something," Tyler said.

"What?" Monica asked.

He didn't answer, but said, "Help him."

The woman knelt down next to Addison. "What can I do?"

Addison suddenly felt angry. "You promised to tell no one," she said.

"I won't tell a soul."

CHAPTER

Seventeen

I returned from sunny Arizona to the gray winter inversion of Utah. It was like the opposite of The Wizard of Oz— from Technicolor to black and white.

✦ NATHAN HURST'S JOURNAL ✦

Dr. Elisabeth Kübler-Ross, the noted psychiatrist and scientist, defined the five stages of loss and grief in this order: denial, anger, bargaining, depression, and acceptance. While we usually think of these stages in terms of death, they apply to all loss. In my breakup with Addison, I was moving through the stages pretty quickly. At first I couldn't believe we were over. We had only just begun. I fully expected to hear from her a few days later when things had calmed down. When after a week she still hadn't called, I knew it was real, and I moved on to phase two: anger—though, in truth, I didn't stay there long. It was difficult to stay angry with Addison when I knew why she had broken up with me.

Stage three, the bargaining phase, was nearly as short-lived as phase two. The only things I had to bargain with was my love, which she'd rejected, and privileged information about her son—something I would never divulge, no matter how desperate I was. So, in a matter of days, I just moved on to depression.

I returned from Arizona to the gray winter inversion of Utah. It seemed appropriate for my state of mind.

I'm not sure why I didn't just jump ahead on to the last

phase: acceptance. As much as I wanted our relationship to last, I had never really expected it. The milk carton thing.

Existential philosophy holds that the worst thing placed in Pandora's box was hope. In my darker moments, I have believed that's true of the human heart as well. But I didn't now. I had seen a miracle in Addison's little boy, and had been a recipient of his remarkable gift. If ever there was a time for hope in my life, it was now. I found myself wondering about Addison and how she and her family were doing.

Neither of us could have known that the course of events already set in place would soon bring us back together.

CHAPTER

Eighteen

*Sometimes I wonder if it's not so much that
we intend to do harm as we don't intend not to.*

✦NATHAN HURST'S JOURNAL✦

Collin slept nearly eighteen hours straight the night he healed Tyler Pyranovich. Four days later he still hadn't the strength to get out of bed. On the fifth day, Addison called his cardiologist. She wasn't sure what to say when he asked if anything had precipitated Collin's sudden decline. Outside of fatigue, which was hardly unusual for a leukemia patient, Collin wasn't showing any other signs of distress. Addison made an appointment for the next week, agreeing to bring him in immediately if he showed any further signs of deterioration.

Addison put Collin in her own bed so she could keep a constant eye on him. During that time, she never stopped berating herself for putting her son in harm's way. To her relief, on the morning of the sixth day, he started to show signs of improvement; his pale complexion warmed with color.

It was early afternoon when a small, balding man came to her door.

"Mrs. Park, I'm Dr. Pyranovich."

Addison was angry when she realized who he was. "What do you want?" She asked gruffly.

"Your boy healed my son."

Addison just glared at him.

"My wife said you made her promise not to tell anyone."

"Then she lied to me."

"I'm sorry. It's Addison, right?"

Addison didn't confirm the question. She just wanted him gone.

"I thought you'd like to know my son went golfing today. Just last week I thought we might be burying him." He looked at her. "What happened is truly a miracle. My son is cured."

"I'm very happy for you. My son's not." She started to shut the door.

"Please. I understand that you're upset. I'm only here to see if there is anything I can do for you or your son."

"My son is too weak to get out of bed. He has a congenital heart defect and is recovering from leukemia. We took a chance helping your son, and it almost killed mine. And to thank us, your wife broke her promise. If you're truly grateful, you'll leave us alone and make sure no one else finds out."

"I'm very sorry. Of course." He hesitated. "Please don't take this wrong, but I don't know how you thought that would be possible. There have been a lot of people watching over my son. He has scores of friends. Everyone at the hospital is talking about his miraculous recovery."

Addison erupted. "Don't you understand? Healing your son almost cost me mine. If everyone knows what he can do, they'll come after him, just like your wife did. The next time he heals someone it could kill him. Tell everyone you've discovered some new cancer cure, I don't care. Just don't tell them about my son."

"I understand," he said sincerely. "I'm sorry. I really am." He looked down. "I really do appreciate your sacrifice and your son's. I wanted you to know I opened a trust fund for your son today. I'd like to pay for his college education. It's nothing compared to the gift he's given us. But we are grateful."

Addison was taken aback by the generosity of the gift. Her voice softened. "Let's just pray he lives long enough to use it."

"I'm very sorry that your son is sick. For the record, it wasn't my wife who told me. It was my son. Understandably, he's pretty excited. I'll have a word with him. We'll do our best to keep the talk down. But when you part the Red Sea, there's going to be a lot of fishermen who want to know what happened."

Addison didn't respond.

"God bless you and your beautiful son. And thank you for giving me back mine. I'll never forget." He turned and slowly walked down the snow-covered walkway to his car. Addison shut the door, locked it, then went to check on Collin.

CHAPTER

Nineteen

Sunsets, like childhood, are viewed with wonder not just because they are beautiful but because they are fleeting.

✦NATHAN HURST'S JOURNAL✦

Addison sat quietly on the side of Collin's bed just looking at her boy. He was sleeping again. He looked peaceful, and this brought her peace as well. When he was a baby, she would hold him for hours, marveling at the miracle he was and wondering for how long he was on loan from God.

After a half hour, his eyes fluttered, and he looked at his mother. She smiled at him. "Hi, baby."

"Hi."

She ran her hand across his cheek. "How are you feeling?"

"Fine."

"A little while ago, Tyler's father came over to thank you. He says Tyler's all better. You saved his life."

"That's good."

Addison gazed at him, full of admiration. "Yes, that's good." She kissed him on the forehead. "I need to pick up Lizzy at the bus stop. Will you be okay alone for a few minutes?"

"Yeah."

"I'll be right back."

The bus was a few minutes late, and Addison was checking her watch for the fifth time when it rounded the corner and plowed through the slush to its corner stop. Elizabeth was the first child off, bounding from the bus with her usual energy.

"Hi, Mom!"

"Hi, sweetie."

"Can Collin play?"

"No, honey, he's still very sick."

Elizabeth frowned. Half way to their home she asked, "When is Mr. Hurst going to come over again?"

"I don't know."

"I think he's nice."

"Yes, he is."

"Did he leave like Daddy?"

"No, honey."

"Did you tell him to go away?"

"That's none of your business."

"Does that mean you did?"

"That means, it's none of your business. And when we get home you need to practice the piano. You have your lesson tomorrow."

"Aw."

As they walked into the house, the phone was ringing. Addison was expecting a call from the pharmacy and hurried to answer it. "Hello."

A young, female voice said, "I'm calling for Mrs. Park."

"This is she."

"Mrs. Park, my name is Gretchen Anderson. I'm calling from the *Salt Lake Tribune*."

"I'm sorry, I cancelled the paper because I just never got around to reading it."

The woman chuckled. "I'm not with circulation. I'm a reporter. A friend of mine is an oncologist at Salt Lake Regional Hospital. One of his patients experienced the most miraculous remission he's seen in his thirty-year practice."

"What does that have to do with me?"

"According to the doctor, your son healed him."

"I don't know what you're talking about."

"Mrs. Park, I've already interviewed Tyler Pyranovich. I know all about your son and his remarkable gift. The story's mostly written. We have extraordinary before and after photographs of Tyler. I'm just calling to check some facts. And, if it's possible, I would like to interview your son."

"No, you may not talk to him. You can't write about him either."

"Mrs. Park, this is an important story. What's happening here . . ."

"We just want to be left alone."

Addison hung up the phone. She could feel a stress headache coming on. She put her fingers on her temples and lightly rubbed them. She waited until she had calmed down, then got a glass of water from the kitchen sink and went into Collin's room.

"Hey, little man, it's time for your medicine." She took the pill case from the dresser and dumped three pills into the palm of her hand. "Here you go."

Collin took the pills and swallowed them, then looked at Addison quizzically. "How come you're afraid?"

"I'm not afraid."

Collin just looked at her.

"Okay. I'm a little worried."

"About what?"

She could see her anxiety mirrored on her son's face.

"Just silly things, baby. Silly things."

CHAPTER

Twenty

There are moments—a phone call, a knock on the door—
when the course of our life changes in a heartbeat,
bringing us what we do not want, and cannot stop.

✦ NATHAN HURST'S JOURNAL ✦

Addison woke to the doorbell. Her first thought was that she had accidentally slept in, until she noticed that there was no light filtering in through the slats in the blinds. She looked at the radio alarm clock and saw that it wasn't even half past five. In the gray delirium between sleep and consciousness, she decided she had only dreamed the sound. She rolled back over to go to sleep, when the doorbell rang again. Then she heard Goldie barking wildly. She sat up and rubbed her eyes. *Who could possibly be at her door at this hour?*

She pulled on her robe, then flipped on the hall light and made her way to the front door. She walked briskly, hoping that whoever it was wouldn't ring again and wake the children.

Goldie was growling and running in a circle in front of the door.

"Quiet, Goldie."

Keeping the security chain attached, Addison unlocked the deadbolt and started to open the door. Before she could open it fully, someone threw themselves against the door, pushing it back until the chain caught. Addison screamed. A hand reached through the space and a woman shouted, "Please, help us. You've got to help us."

The woman pushed her face into the space between the door and its frame. "My baby's sick. Your son can heal her. Please, help us."

Addison stepped back from the door. A car's headlights tracked across the picture window, illuminating the room.

"Please. Just have your boy stick his hand out and touch her . . ."

"Go away!" Addison shouted. She tried to push the door shut but couldn't, so she left it, watching the woman's arm move around inside her house.

There were suddenly enlarged silhouettes of people against the front curtains. She pulled the curtain back just enough to see a group of people congregating in her front yard. Elizabeth stumbled into the room, holding a stuffed bear in one arm and rubbing her eyes. "Mommy, there's people talking outside."

Addison gathered her in her arms. "Come here, honey." She carried Elizabeth into her room, where Collin was still sleeping. She locked the door. And then she called me.

CHAPTER

Twenty-One

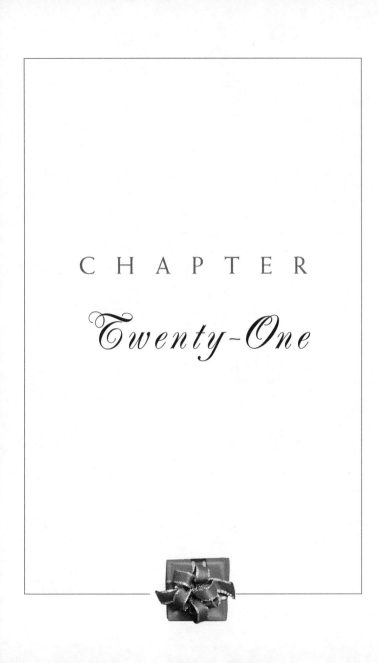

Collin has been discovered.

✶ NATHAN HURST'S JOURNAL ✶

I had set my alarm that morning for six thirty as I was scheduled to be on a plane by nine, headed for Louisville. I had been up until two in the morning, finishing a book, and hadn't been able to stop thinking about the story, so I had only been asleep a couple hours when my cell phone rang. It had been charging by the side of my bed, and I lifted it by the charger's cord. "Yeah?"

Addison's voice came tight and panicked. "Nathan, it's Addison."

"Addison?"

"I'm sorry to call so early. I didn't know who else to turn to. I need your help."

I was wide awake immediately. "What's wrong?"

"My yard is filled with people. They're trying to get in my house."

It was difficult to comprehend what she was saying. "What people?"

"I think a newspaper story's been written about Collin."

"How many people are there?"

"I don't know. Maybe a dozen. Maybe more. I don't know what to do."

"Have you called the police?"

"No. Not yet. I'm sorry to wake you. Are you in town?"

"Yeah. I'll be right over. I'll call the police on my way. Just make sure all your doors are locked, and keep away from the windows."

"Please hurry."

"I'm on my way. Try to stay calm. Collin and Elizabeth need you to be calm."

"Okay," she said, breathing out. "Okay, I can do that."

"I'm going to hang up now to call the police. Call me immediately if anything happens."

⋆

I quickly pulled on some jeans and a sweatshirt and hurried out to my car in the frigid morning air. My windshield was frosted over, and I scraped it just enough for visibility, then hopped in and started the car. I dialed 911 as I waited for the window to clear. "I need the police."

"What's the problem, sir?"

"My friend's house is surrounded by a mob of people. I'm afraid they might break in."

"How many people?"

"At least a dozen or more. She wasn't sure."

"Are these people armed?"

"I don't know."

"What is the address of the house?"

"It's in Murray. I believe it's 5412 Walden. It's the home of Addison Park."

"Are you at the house?"

"No, I'm headed over there right now. She just called me."

"What is your name, sir?"

"It's Nathan Hurst. Just send the police."

"The police have been dispatched, sir. Why would people surround her house?"

"There was an article in the paper . . . Just hurry." I hung up the phone. What was I going to say? Her son can magically heal people and everyone wants a piece of him? And he's holed up with Elvis and the Easter Bunny?

The sun was just peeking above the mountains when I pulled into Addison's neighborhood. Addison had underestimated the size of the crowd; there were at least sixty people. Cars lined both sides of the street. The police were already on the scene, herding people off the lawn and away from her home. An officer yelled at me as I pulled into her driveway.

"Pull out of the driveway, sir." His hand rested on the club still in his holster belt.

I'd worked too closely with police to be intimidated. I rolled down my window. "I'm Nate Hurst. I'm a friend of the family."

"You're going to have to back out of the driveway, sir."

I put my car in park, shut it off, and stepped out, glancing at his badge. "Captain Johnson, I'm the one who called 911."

The officer followed me as I walked up to the porch. A few of the onlookers saw me and tried to follow. I stopped and turned on them. "Go away!" I shouted, my words exploding into clouds in the frigid air. "Get out of here."

An officer stood guarding the door, his arms crossed in front of him. "I'm a friend," I told him, "Mrs. Park is expecting me."

"I'll have to verify that, sir. What's your name?"

"It's Nathan."

"Nathan what?"

"Nathan Hurst."

I stood on the porch as he went in. Only then did I wonder why I hadn't brought a coat. He returned seconds later. "You can come in."

There were several other officers inside the house standing around Addison and talking to her. Addison turned to me, and I saw a wave of relief cross her face.

"Nathan."

We met halfway across the living room and embraced.

"Are you okay?" I asked.

"I'm so glad you're here."

For a moment I just held her.

"This is just crazy," she said. "I can't believe it."

"How did this happen?"

"Collin cured a teenager of cancer and it made the news. His mother promised she wouldn't tell anyone, but . . . I never should have let him do it . . . It made him so sick."

"What are the police telling you to do?"

"They say we need to get Collin out of here. But I'm not sure where to go."

I thought about it. "My apartment's too small. But there's one of those extended stay hotels near my home."

I walked over and looked out the window. Cars were moving slowly up and down the road. The police had stretched a line of yellow police tape across the front of the yard, and Addison's home now had the appearance of a crime scene. A television news van had stopped out front, and a woman reporter was interviewing people standing outside the yellow line.

"Looks like the television news is here."

One of the police officers approached us. "Mrs. Park, we're doing our best to disperse the crowd, but more people are coming. We think it's best that you get your kids away from here as soon as possible."

"We were thinking they could stay at a hotel for a few days," I said.

Addison asked the officer, "After we go, will you leave?"

"No, ma'am. We'll leave a patrol car here for a day or two. People go nuts over these kinds of things. They might try to break in and take something of your son's or sleep in his bed or do something crazy. We're supposed to get some snow tomorrow, so that should help keep the crowd down."

Addison frowned. "You think people will still be here tomorrow?"

"We've no way of knowing, ma'am. But if your son isn't here, there's no reason for them to stay."

"What's the best way to get him out of here?" Addison asked.

"It's best if we get him out first and then let the crowd know he's gone."

"The back seat of my car folds down into the trunk," I said. "Collin can lie back there until we're out of the neighborhood. I'll drive around until I'm sure we're not being followed, then take him to the hotel. You and Elizabeth can pack your things and meet us this afternoon."

"A trunk?" Addison asked.

"It's not really a trunk, it's just covered. He'll be okay."

"Sounds reasonable," the officer said.

Addison took a deep breath. "Okay. I'll pack some things for him." Addison turned to go then suddenly stopped. She looked me in the eyes. "Thank you for coming. I missed you."

I smiled. No matter the reason, I was glad to be back.

CHAPTER

Twenty-Two

Today, Addison told me that she loves me. I wasn't sure how to respond. I haven't much experience with that sort of thing.

✦NATHAN HURST'S JOURNAL ✦

I went outside and pulled my car into the garage, next to Addison's, then shut the garage door. I entered the house through the interior door. Collin was in his room, lying on top of his bed playing Nintendo. Elizabeth sat on the floor in front of him, watching and cheering. She looked up as I entered. She was excited to see me.

"Mr. Hurst, I don't have to go to school today," she said.

"Every cloud has a silver lining," I replied.

"What does that mean?"

I winked at her. "It means you don't have to go to school today." I turned to Collin. "Did your mom tell you we're leaving?"

"Yeah. Can I take my Nintendo?"

"I'm not going anywhere without the Nintendo," I said.

He smiled, then shut off the game. Addison walked into the room with a small suitcase. "Here are some of Collin's things. I also packed his medication. Some of it needs to be taken on a full stomach. It's important that he gets everything at the right time. I've put in a copy of the schedule, and I'll call to remind you.

I unzipped the suitcase to see what we had. Inside were

several changes of clothes, a few books, and a transparent pill case with slots for each day of the week. There was also a plastic bag filled with plastic medicine bottles and a folded piece of paper that I assumed was the schedule. I counted twelve different medications. More than I expected.

"How long do you think you'll be?" I asked.

"It will take a few hours to pack everything we need. And I still need to find someone to take Goldie." She opened the pill case and spilled two pills into the palm of her hand. "He'll need these before nine. He should take them with break-fast."

I put them in my pocket. "Okay. I'll get us checked in and we'll see you later."

Addison stepped close to me, speaking only slightly above a whisper. "Be careful with him. He only got out of bed yesterday for the first time. He shouldn't climb stairs."

"I'll take care of him."

She kissed me on my cheek, then crouched down next to Collin. "I'll see you in a little bit. Until then be sure to do whatever Mr. Hurst says."

"Okay. Bye, Mom," Collin said, hugging her.

"I love you."

"I love you too."

She walked us to the door. She put her hand in mine. "Nathan, I love you too."

It was the first time I'd heard those words since I was eight.

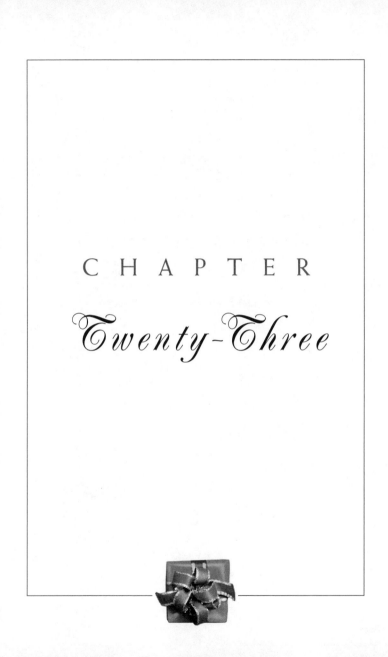

CHAPTER

Twenty-Three

It's been said, a minute on the other side of the veil would be of more value than every book on religion ever written. I believe that is true.

⁜NATHAN HURST'S JOURNAL⁜

The police pulled back the yellow tape as I slowly backed out of the driveway. A few people strained to look inside my car, but I have tinted windows, and for the most part people kept their distance. As I drove out of the neighborhood, I checked my mirrors to see if anyone had followed us. A Cadillac Escalade turned out after us, but it was more likely coincidence than stalking. It trailed us for about six blocks, then turned off on State Street. About ten minutes after we left the neighborhood, I pulled into a gas station. "I think we're safe," I said. "How are you doing?" I glanced in the rearview mirror. The blanket rose, and Collin pulled it off his head. He looked pale.

"You okay?"

"Yeah."

"Let's put the seat up." I climbed out of the car and walked around to the back. Collin slowly got out. He leaned against the car as I pulled up the back seat.

"There you go," I said.

Collin bent over and threw up. I walked over and put my hand on his back. He vomited several more times; finally he seemed to be done. I got some tissues from my glove box and handed them to him. He wiped his mouth.

"You okay?" I asked.

He nodded, looking down at the mess on the ground. I could tell it bothered him.

"Don't worry about it. I used to drink a lot. It happened to me all the time." I opened his door, then got in my own seat and started the car. "Well, partner, we're on the lam."

"A lamb?"

"*L-A-M.* It means we're fugitives."

It was all lost on him. "When is my mom coming?"

"This afternoon."

He was quiet for several minutes. Then he asked, "Am I in trouble?"

I glanced at him in the mirror. "No, of course not."

"What did those people want?"

It had never occurred to me that Collin didn't really know what was happening.

"There was a story in the newspaper about you this morning."

He looked both excited and doubtful. "Really?"

"That teenage boy you cured told some people about you. That's why the people came. They wanted you to heal them."

"Were they all sick?"

"Just some of them. Most of them just care about someone who is sick. Like your mom cares about you."

"How come my mom was afraid of them?"

"I think she was afraid they would make you sick."

I could tell he was thinking this through. "I wish she were here."

"Me too, pal." I drove a few minutes more, still checking my rearview mirror. I pulled into a Starbucks drive-in lane. I called Miche as I waited to order. I caught her as she was about to leave for work.

"Miche, it's Nate."

There was a hesitation. "I hope you're calling from the airport."

"Yeah, there's been a change of plans. Something's come up."

"Huh?"

I wasn't surprised at her reaction. In all the time we'd worked together, I'd never missed an engagement.

"I need you to do something for me."

"What do you need?"

"There's an extended stay hotel near my apartment around Twenty-first and Highland Drive. I don't remember the name. Do you know the one I'm talking about?"

"Yes. By that steak house."

"Right. Just a minute." The car ahead of me had pulled forward, and I drove up to the speaker box. "I'd like a black coffee, venti." I turned back to Collin. "You want a hot chocolate?"

He shook his head.

"How about some water?"

He nodded.

"And a bottle of water." I put the phone back to my ear. "I'm back. I need you to go to the hotel and reserve two rooms in my name. Make sure they're connected and on the ground level, if possible."

"For how long?"

"Make it a week. Put it on my credit card."

"Your business card?"

"No, my personal one. Just a minute."

I pulled forward and got our drinks. I slid mine into my cup holder and handed Collin his water. "Sorry, where were we?"

"I'm getting two connecting rooms on the ground floor for one week and putting them on your credit card."

"Right. Then get the keys. Make sure that you don't tell anyone where I am."

"This is getting weird. Does this have anything to do with Addison's son?"

"How did you know that?"

"I read the article in the *Tribune*."

"You weren't the only one."

"Is it true? Can he really heal people?"

"Remember when I came back from Denver and my bronchitis was gone?"

"I *knew* there was something fishy about that. Wow, that's incredible. Should I meet you at the hotel?"

"No. We'll meet somewhere else just in case I'm being followed. You know that Home Depot on Twenty-first and Third? I'll meet you there."

"Are you in some kind of trouble?"

"Not exactly. Things are just a little complicated. Oh, and pick up a copy of today's newspaper on the way. I want to read that article."

"I'll bring mine. What should I tell Stayner?"

"Tell him I'm taking a few sick days."

"Got it. I'll call when I'm leaving the hotel."

I stowed my phone in an empty cup holder. "Hey, look, Collin, the golden arches. Want to go to McDonald's?"

"Yes, please. Can we go inside? There's a playground."

"Sorry, I don't think we should." I pulled in behind another car in the drive-through. "What would you like?"

"A Happy Meal with chicken nuggets."

"I think they just have breakfast. How about a pancake meal?"

"Okay."

We got our food and a copy of *USA Today*. As we pulled from the drive-through window, I saw that there were only a few people seated inside. I was tempted to let Collin go in, but then I saw someone reading a paper and thought better of it. I didn't know if Collin's story ran with pictures.

I parked in a deserted corner of the parking lot where the plows had pushed the snow into five-foot banks. The temperature outside had still not climbed above freezing, and I left the car running with the heater on. I flipped through my paper as I ate my sausage biscuit. There was a front-page article on the dismal shape of America's health system, with a graph showing how many people were unable to afford adequate healthcare. *If only we could clone Collin*, I thought. It occurred to me that someone would want to try. Collin sat quietly in the back seat, dipping pieces of pancake in a small plastic container of syrup. I remembered his pills and fished them from my pocket.

"Hey, your mom said to take these with your breakfast."

He put them in his mouth and swallowed them with a drink of orange juice.

"I couldn't even swallow pills when I was your age."

He just cut another piece of pancake.

"What does it feel like when you heal someone?"

He shrugged.

"Does it make you tired?"

"Yeah." He looked back down at his breakfast. "Anyone can do it."

"No, I don't think so. You're pretty special."

"They just don't know they can. You know when you cut yourself, and your mom kisses it better? It's like that."

"I don't think it's that easy," I said. "I think there are a lot of parents who would give anything to heal their children." Collin didn't answer. "So, when did you know you could heal?"

"When I was in the *other place*, they told me."

"What other place?"

"You know. When I died."

"Who told you?"

"The people."

"People? You mean . . . like angels?"

"They're just people. They don't have wings."

I suddenly realized the singular opportunity I had. For millennia mankind had wondered what, if anything, existed beyond the grave. In the back seat of my Subaru, I had someone who had actually been there—sort of a Marco Polo of the afterlife. "What was the *other place* like?" I asked.

Collin thought for a moment. "It's hard to describe. There

were a lot of colors we don't have here. But it's like everything is alive, like trees and bushes and stuff."

"Trees are alive here too," I said.

"I know. But you can't talk to them."

"You can talk to trees there?"

He looked as if he wasn't sure how to answer. "Not really talk. You just kind of know what they're thinking."

Trees think?

Addison was right in fearing for Collin's safety. One appearance on *The Today Show*, and Collin could sell a million books. He could start a religion and people would flock by the thousands. Tens of thousands. *In the land of the blind the one-eyed man is king.*

"Was the *other place* heaven?"

"I don't know."

"Is there a hell?"

He said something I've pondered at least a thousand times since. "I don't know." Then he added, "I think maybe it's here."

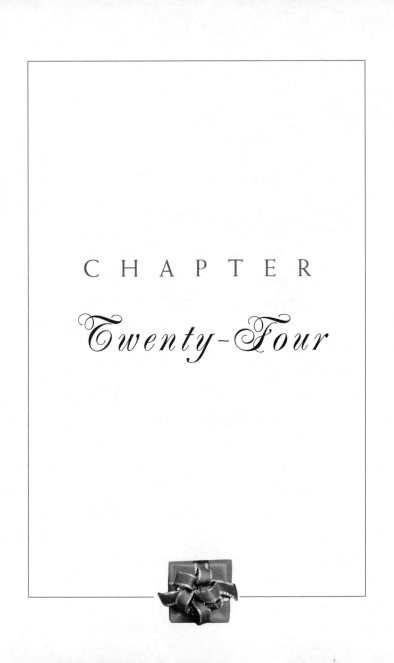

CHAPTER

Twenty-Four

Collin is a little boy with his feet in two worlds.

✦ NATHAN HURST'S JOURNAL ✦

I was sitting there sipping my coffee and thinking about our conversation when my thoughts were interrupted by my phone. I glanced at the caller ID. It was Miche.

"Mission accomplished, boss. I'm headed to the rendezvous."

"You're enjoying this, aren't you?"

"How could you tell?"

"We're on our way. See you in ten minutes."

I turned onto the road while Collin was still finishing his meal.

"So, Christmas is less than two weeks away. Have you decided what you want from Santa?"

"A Samantha doll."

It wasn't what I expected to hear. "I thought you'd want a new Nintendo game. Do a lot of boys play with dolls these days?"

"Not for me. For Lizzy."

"Of course." I admit I was a little relieved to hear this. "What do *you* want?"

He put the styrofoam platter back in the sack, then pushed it to the other side of the seat. "I don't want anything."

"You've got to want something."

"Why?"

"Because kids want things."

"I don't want anything. But Lizzy's gonna need that doll after I'm gone."

I glanced at him in the mirror. "Where are you going?"

He looked as if he were embarrassed to say. "Back."

"Back where?"

"The *other place*." He said this as casually as if he were going on vacation.

"You shouldn't talk that way," I said. "You're going to get all better."

"Grandpa told me I wouldn't."

"Grandpa? But your grandpa . . ." I stopped myself. "You've seen your grandpa?"

"Yeah."

"When?"

"A lot of times."

"When was the last time you saw him?"

"Last night. He came to tell me about all the people who would come today. He said I'd be getting sicker, but it was just for a while, and then I would go stay with him and Grandma, and I wouldn't ever get sick again. He said Mom and Lizzy won't be coming for a while, but not to worry because I can see them whenever I want."

My heart felt like it was pounding out of my chest. "Did he say when you'd be going?"

"Yeah."

"Can you tell me?"

"I'm not supposed to say."

"Is it before Christmas?"

"Yeah."

My chest hurt. "Have you told your mother about this?"

"No."

"Are you going to tell her?"

He looked uncomfortable with the question. "Grandpa says it's best not to tell her."

"But don't you think she should know?"

"I promised I wouldn't tell. Please don't tell her." He looked at me fearfully. "Please."

After a minute, I slowly exhaled. "All right, I won't."

"Promise?"

I hated to say it. "I promise."

CHAPTER

Twenty-Five

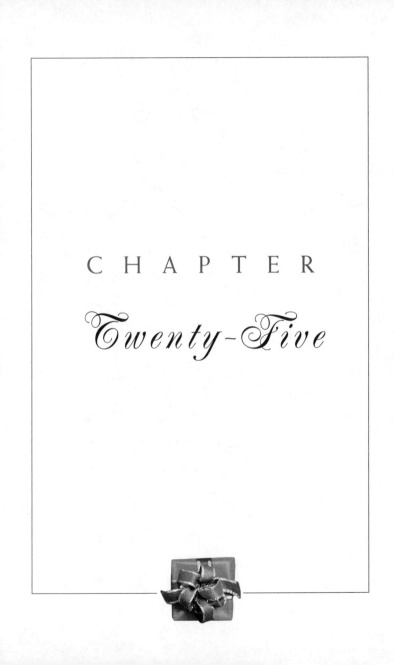

To the thief, everyone's a crook. To the liar, everyone's a fraud.
The curse of all sin is the mirror of false perception it traps us in.

✦ NATHAN HURST'S JOURNAL ✦

"Elizabeth, get away from the window."

"But the people are waving at me."

"You need to finish eating so we can go."

Elizabeth sat back down to her bowl of cereal. "Mommy, when are the people going to leave?"

Addison was kneeling on the kitchen floor putting food into a wheeled suitcase. "I don't know. I wish they would go now."

"How come we don't let them in?"

"Because we don't want them in our house."

"But you get mad at me when I don't let people in."

"We didn't invite these people to our house. We don't want them here."

"Like me, eh?"

Addison turned.

"Daddy!" Elizabeth shouted.

Steve stood in the archway of the kitchen door. He wore a dark European-tailored suit with a bright yellow silk tie; a matching handkerchief, meticulously folded, peeked out of his breast pocket. "Quite a circus you've got going, Addy. You should sell tickets. I had to show ID to some tin-badge deputy to get in."

"What are you doing here?"

Elizabeth ran to him. "Daddy! Did you bring me something?"

"Not this time, *principessa*. But I'll make up for it when we go to Disneyland."

"We're going to Disneyland?"

"This Christmas. If your mom lets you."

"Mom! Can we? Please!"

Addison breathed out in exasperation. "Steve, why do you make promises like that? It gets their hopes up, and then I'm the one who has to deal with their disappointment."

"It's always about you, isn't it?" He crouched down next to Elizabeth. "I plan on taking my two favorite children to Disneyland at Christmas." He smiled at Elizabeth. "Don't you want to see Mickey?"

"Yes! Mommy, can we? I want to see Mickey!"

"What are you doing here, Steve?"

He stood. "I was late for my last visit, so I thought I'd catch up."

"You're *three weeks* late for your last visit."

"I've been busy."

"This wouldn't have something to do with the newspaper story?"

"No, I didn't read the paper today. But I heard the most intriguing interview on the radio. They were interviewing a teenager who had just a few days left to live when he was completely healed of a brain tumor by a little boy. I almost changed the station before he said the boy's name was Collin Park. I nearly choked on my latte."

"And now that he's famous, you want to see him."

"And now that he's famous, you don't want me to see him?"

"The only one keeping you from your son is you. Not even visiting him once during his chemo treatments hardly qualifies you for Father of the Year. You can't see him right now anyway, so please just leave. We're a little busy this morning."

"You can't keep me from my child."

"Children. You have two."

"Just chill, Addy, before you give us both an aneurism. Why are you always so uptight?"

"Collin's not here."

"Nice try."

"Fine, look for yourself."

Steve glared at her suspiciously. "I will." He went to Collin and Elizabeth's bedrooms, then the master bedroom. He returned with a scowl on his face. "Lizzy, where's Collin?"

"He went with Mr. Hurst."

He looked at Addison. "Who's Mr. Hurst?" He walked toward her, noticing for the first time that she was packing things. "What are you doing?"

"Getting away from here. The police told us to leave."

"They can't make you do that."

"They're helping us."

"Where are you going?"

"None of your business."

"Yes, it is."

Addison crouched down and took some bottles from the refrigerator. "What's your angle, Steve?"

"After all these years you still don't trust me."

"I've learned *not* to trust you. How's the bra model?"

He smiled at the reference. "Mia? She's really very nice—and nonjudgmental. You could learn a lot from her. You gals should go to lunch sometime."

"I'll save the date."

"Wow, Addy. Nice comeback. In the olden days, you'd just roll over and play dead."

It was all Addison could do to not throw a can at him. "Elizabeth, go to your room and read."

"I want to stay with Daddy."

Steve smiled triumphantly.

"I wasn't asking. Now go."

Elizabeth looked at her father, who rolled his eyes and made a funny face. "You know how angry Mommy gets. Better go before she blows."

Elizabeth stormed off, stomping her feet in protest. Steve walked to the other side of the counter. "You want an angle? Try this: health care is a trillion-dollar industry. Do you have any idea what people will pay to prolong their lives? Think about it, what good is a hundred million dollars if you're dying? No one takes it with them. People would give it all to live. If we play this right, we'll be richer than God."

"Bravo, Steve. You found a way to pimp our son."

"You make it sound so dirty."

"That's because it is."

"This isn't just about money. This is about the greater good. Think of all the people we can help."

Addison zipped the suitcase shut and stood. "You want to

help people? Open a free clinic for all the poor who can't afford Cadillac health care."

"Same old Addy. No imagination. No dream."

Just then a man pressed his face against the glass of the kitchen window.

Addison hit the glass with the palm of her hand. "Get out of here." She pulled the curtain closed.

"It's just crazy what desperate people will do, isn't it?" Steve said.

"It won't work, Steve. It's not like Collin's handing out autographs. It makes him sick every time he heals someone. If you were ever around, you'd know he's not doing too well."

For the first time, Steve looked concerned. "But he can still do it now and then . . . right?"

"No, he can't."

Steve crossed his arms. "But you decided he was well enough to help that teenager."

"I made a mistake."

"Listen to yourself. You saved a young man's life and it was a mistake." Suddenly his expression changed. "You know, you're looking like you're feeling pretty good yourself. How's your lupus?"

She hesitated. "Just leave."

His mouth pursed. "So that's *your* angle. You got yours, and now you don't care about anyone else." He stepped toward her, his face threatening. "Let me be clear about this. You can't legally stop me from seeing my son." His expression lightened a little. "Besides, I'm just talking about a trip to Disneyland to meet one of my clients, shake hands, have Collin do whatever it is he does, that's it. Bada bing, bada boom. I'll even cut you in for ten percent."

"You know, I used to feel sorry for you. But now you just make me sick."

"Sick, huh? I know someone who can help you with that." He stopped at the kitchen door. "With or without you, I'm going to do the right thing. You want to keep Collin to yourself; well, there are people in this world with life-and-death struggles, and we're going to help them. We'll be their saviors."

"You keep telling yourself that, Steve. The only person you've ever cared about in this world is yourself."

"Then we're more alike than you think." With that he walked out the back door, slamming it behind him.

Addison groaned as the door shut. "Elizabeth!"

Elizabeth walked in, forgetting that she was mad at her mother. "Yes, Mommy?"

"Let's get out of here."

CHAPTER

Twenty-Six

Heroes rarely look the way we draw them in our minds:
attractive, imposing figures with rippling muscles and
strong chins. More times than not they are humble beings:
small and flawed. It is only their spirits
that are beautiful and strong.

✦ NATHAN HURST'S JOURNAL ✦

By the time Collin and I arrived at the Home Depot, Miche's yellow Volkswagen convertible was parked on the east side of the lot, idling in the shadow of a large trailer. I drew up alongside her, and we both killed our engines, getting out of our cars at the same time. It felt like something dodgy was going down.

"Where's your coat?" she asked.

"I forgot it."

"I can run by your place and get it."

"I'll be all right."

"Just don't want you getting sick again. Or maybe that's not a concern anymore."

She handed me the newspaper and two small hotel envelopes. "Here's your paper and your keycards. Sorry, they're on the second floor. They didn't have two adjoining rooms available on the ground floor."

"That's okay. I'll carry him." I slid the envelopes into my pants pocket. "What section is the article in?"

"It's right there. I folded the page back for you."

For all the attention it had generated, the story was relatively brief. There was an interview with Tyler Pyranovich, along with before and after photographs. In this case, the pictures were worth a million words. In the first photograph, the kid looked swollen and bruised, like Rocky Balboa after his first title match. The next picture looked like a headshot from a modeling agency. It was pretty compelling. "No wonder," I said.

"Is he in the car?" Miche asked.

I looked up from the paper. "In the back seat."

"Can I meet him?"

I rolled the paper up then went and opened the back door. Collin was lying sideways playing his Nintendo DS. "Collin, this is Miche. She's my assistant."

He looked up from his game. "Hi," he said shyly.

"Hi. It's nice to meet you. Is that a Nintendo DS?"

"Yeah."

"My husband has one of those."

"An old guy has one?"

She laughed. "Yeah, that's what I said. Old guys shouldn't have these. But he's kind of a geek. It's nice meeting you, Collin."

"Thanks."

She shut the door and took a few steps toward me. "He's just a little boy."

"What did you expect?"

"I don't know. Moses."

I grinned.

"I called the store manager in Louisville. I briefed him on the theft, and he's going to take care of everything."

"Thanks."

"So what now, boss?"

"We're going to hide out for a few days and hope this blows over. There's supposed to be another storm moving in. That should help."

"In the meantime, I better get to work." She smiled. "Hey, I caught a fish. A kid in Nashville specializing in banjo heists."

"You found him yourself?"

She looked pretty proud of herself. "I did."

"Well done. Now I know who'll replace me."

"Oh no. You go, I go." She opened her car door.

"What are you doing Thursday night?" I asked.

"Nothing. Dane's playing Risk with his geek buddies."

"Have you ever babysat?"

"What do you think I do all day?"

"Thanks. So, would you mind watching Collin and his sister while I take Addison out? I'll pay you handsomely."

"You don't have to pay me. Anything else?"

"Not right now. But keep your phone with you."

"I always do. Your rooms are on the east side of the building. Ciao." She looked at Collin and waved. He waved back.

She shook her head in wonder. "He's just a kid."

CHAPTER

Twenty-Seven

Today I spoke with my brother.

✦ NATHAN HURST'S JOURNAL ✦

In the few minutes it took to reach the hotel, Collin had already fallen asleep. I parked near our rooms, then leaned back over the seat and gently woke him. "Hey, bud. We're here."

His eyes opened slowly. "Where are we?"

"We're at a hotel. I'm going to check our room." I ran up the stairs and unlocked one of the suites, propping the door open with the latch lock, then hurried back down. "I'm going to carry you up, okay?"

"Sure."

I slid my arms under him. He couldn't have weighed more than eighty pounds, and I easily climbed the stairs with him in my arms. I lay him down on the couch in the front room, then went back down to the car to bring up his suitcase. When I was finished, I sat down on a chair next to him. "You doing okay?"

He nodded even though he looked like he was in pain.

"Do you need to throw up again?"

"No."

"Want me to turn on the TV?"

He shook his head. He had a peculiar blank look on his face. "Who's Tommy?" he asked softly.

The question stunned me.

"How do you know that name?" I asked forcefully.

Collin looked at me anxiously.

"I'm sorry," I said more calmly. "How do you know that name?"

"It's his name." He pointed behind me. Chills went down my spine. I turned but saw nothing. I knelt down next to Collin. "Do you see Tommy?"

He nodded.

I looked again to where he had pointed. "There's no one there," I said, as if trying to convince myself. My heart pounded fiercely. I didn't want to believe him. But how could he have known about Tommy? Addison didn't even know about Tommy.

"If he's here," I said, "he's going to have to prove it."

"He's there," Collin said, pointing a yard to my left.

"The morning when . . . Christmas morning, we were playing big game hunters. We were hunting a tiger. What was its name?"

I don't know if I expected to hear or feel something or what, but nothing happened. After a moment, I turned back to Collin. "I didn't hear anything," I said.

Collin rubbed his face. "He said its name was Sandy Claws."

I shivered, though the room wasn't cold. My brother was with me. I suddenly felt sick to my stomach. When I could speak, I said, "Collin, tell him I'm sorry. I am so sorry."

"He can hear you."

I looked back to the vacant space that was my brother. "Why can't I see you?" I held out my hand. It was trembling. "Tommy, touch my hand." I felt nothing. "Collin?"

"He said you can't feel him," Collin said matter-of-factly.

"Does he know I'm sorry?"

There was a long pause. "He says it's time to stop being sorry."

My eyes welled up with tears. "How do I do that, Tommy? How do I stop being sorry?"

When Collin answered, I knew he spoke someone else's words. "Free Mom. Free yourself."

CHAPTER

Twenty-Eight

*I believe that the difference between Heaven and Hell
is not so much the climate as the company.
Living in a world populated by people like themselves would,
for many, be Heaven. And for others, it would, indeed, be Hell.*

✦ NATHAN HURST'S JOURNAL ✦

After leaving Addison's house, Steve stopped at the first grocery store he passed. He put two quarters in the newspaper box in front of the store and took the entire stack of papers inside. When he got to his office, he dropped a copy of Collin's story on his secretary's desk, instructing her to make two hundred color copies and to hold his calls. He spent the next four hours on the phone with various newspapers and radio stations scheduling interviews. It was a simple rule of economics: *The greater the demand, the higher the price.*

Around four o'clock he made a house call to the home of Mr. Riley Franzen, one of the firm's most valued clients.

The Franzen home was a seven-million-dollar colonial-style mansion nestled in the foothill of Capitol Hill. It was a behemoth of an estate, nearly fifteen thousand square feet, not including the two vacant guest houses. Riley Franzen had made his money in real estate, developing high-end shopping centers and strip malls. He was sixty-eight, though his body was functioning more like a ninety-year-old's from the effect of his vices. From his first million on, his life had been one of luxuriant excess: expensive women, drink, and cigars. Consequently, he suffered from emphysema, heart disease, and the most pressing of his afflictions, stage four liver failure. In the last few months he had developed ascites, an accumulation of fluid in his abdominal cavity, which had caused his belly to swell until he looked like he was eight months pregnant with twins.

Even with money and clout, his obesity and the condition of his heart and lungs made him an unlikely candidate for a liver transplant. His doctors didn't think he'd survive the surgery or tolerate the drug regimen after, and they couldn't ethically risk losing a patient and a healthy organ.

Franzen had located a discreet clinic in Switzerland that provided organs at a price for wealthy patrons. While the origins of the donor organs were questionable at best, he had made arrangements for the trip. In the meantime, he had engaged his law firm in the preparation of a final will, just in case. In truth, the purpose of Franzen's will was less to ensure who would get his money than who would not.

Franzen's nurse led Steve back to the sunroom. Steve hadn't seen Franzen for several weeks, and he was amazed at how much his client had deteriorated in such a short time. His first thought was that Franzen looked a little like a pregnant Papa Hemingway, with his white beard framing a long, unlit cigar. The steady draw and click from Franzen's oxygen tank reverberated in the tile-floored room. He sat at a glass table doing a crossword puzzle, a teacup and teapot in front of him.

"Good afternoon, Mr. Franzen," Steve said, setting down his leather portfolio.

Franzen spoke with the cigar still in his mouth. "For someone." Franzen was cantankerous by nature, but his deteriorating health had made him more so.

"If my day were any better, I'd have to kill myself."

Franzen took the cigar from his mouth. "I don't know what that means, but as long as you leave me your liver I won't stop you."

Steve pulled out a chair and sat down at the table. Franzen put the cigar back in his mouth then went back to his puzzle. "So, I take it you finally got around to my will," he said gruffly. "What's a six letter word for 'burning'?"

"I don't know. I'm not good at those things."

"You're not much good at your lawyering either. My will should have been completed weeks ago."

"It's almost done."

Franzen looked up, his eyes fierce. "You're *still* not done? Then why are you wasting my time?"

"I came across something I'm certain you'll be interested in." Steve handed him the paper folded back to expose the article about Collin. "Did you see this story?"

"Haven't read anything but *The Wall Street Journal* for years."

"You'll want to read this." Steve tapped the article.

The photographs caught Franzen's eye. He pushed his glasses further up the bridge of his nose and lifted the paper to read the article. When he was done, he looked up at Steve. "Do you know this boy?"

Steve smiled. "He's my son."

Franzen sat back in his chair, champing down on the cigar with his back teeth. "Really?"

"Collin lives with my ex. You should see what's going on at the house. It's like the Rose Parade, only the float stays and the crowd drives by. People are flying in from all over the world." Steve leaned forward, his voice falling dramatically. "People are offering their fortunes just to be touched by him."

"All that from this morning's article in the *Salt Lake Tribune*," Franzen said skeptically.

"Of course not. It's on the Internet."

Franzen glanced down at the paper again. "Can you get me to him?"

Steve could see the desperation in the old man's eyes, and it thrilled him. "Well, that's what I'm here to negotiate," he said, affecting a disinterested air. "I suppose that with the right incentive, all things are possible."

His lawyer's sudden impudence infuriated Franzen. "I'm one of the original clients of Hardy Nelsen. I was with the firm when you were still in diapers."

"And now *you're* in diapers."

Franzen's face reddened. "You insolent son of—"

Steve cut him off. "Can it, Franzen. I'm done with the day job. And I'm through kowtowing to you or anyone else. I know the value of what I've got here. I can make as much in an hour as the entire firm makes in a year, which means I can retire richer than God by three o'clock tomorrow. But if you're not interested." Steve stood, lifting his briefcase. "It's your funeral." He turned his back on Franzen and began to walk away.

Franzen took the cigar from his mouth and placed it on the table. "Wait, Park. Let's talk."

Steve paused midstep, a nearly indiscernible smile crossing his lips. Then he turned and looked at the old man. "Frankly, Riley, I was rewarding our association by offering the first opening to you." Steve returned to the table deliciously in control. "Just so you understand the scope of this, I've got sheiks from the United Arab Emirates who want to send a private jet for my boy. That's pretty rich company, even for you. It's all about supply and demand. Millions of people looking for a cure and there's only one source." Steve sat down, laying his briefcase between them. "Unfortunately, my son can only do so many healings a year, and you know better than anyone that scarcity drives the value of everything. Ever since this piece hit, the offers are coming thick and fast. It comes down to highest bidder. I'm offering you the inside track."

"My kingdom for a horse," Franzen said softly.

"I'm not asking for the whole kingdom. Just a corner of what you've already signed away." Steve opened his briefcase. "I've spent the last three weeks looking at all that money you're planning to leave to ungrateful, lazy step-children who you don't care for, ex-wives you can't stand, and greedy charities you don't really care about. It's your money. You should use it for *you*." Steve lifted the cigar from the table. "You always had a taste for fine things. Especially cigars. Imagine being able to light one again." He looked Franzen in the eyes. "The real question is, what's it worth to you?"

CHAPTER

Twenty-Nine

It is one thing to take joy in a child's achievements and quite another to aggrandize ourselves through them. It is emotional incest to live vicariously through a child's success.

✦ NATHAN HURST'S JOURNAL ✦

I was still considerably shaken by the experience with Tommy when Addison and Elizabeth arrived. Addison's arms were full of bags. Elizabeth had a small backpack over one shoulder, and she carried a stuffed giraffe under her arm.

"Let me give you a hand," I said, taking the bags from Addison.

"Thanks." She kissed my cheek. "Where's Collin?"

"He's in the bedroom, sleeping. Do you have anything else in the car?"

"There are a couple more bags. They're heavy. At least for me."

I went down to her car and brought the rest of her bags up. When I returned, she was standing in the kitchen looking in the small closet next to the refrigerator.

"What have you got in these suitcases? Lead?"

"Sorry, it's food. Just set them over here. I wasn't sure how long we'd be here, so I kind of emptied the cupboards." She unzipped the suitcase and began transferring the contents to the pantry. I crouched down to help her. "Here, I'll hand you things."

"Thanks."

"So, I gather from the amount of food you brought that the crowd's still there."

"It's grown."

"How did your escape go?"

"That was exciting. At least six people followed me. When I stopped at the light on the Seventy-second off-ramp, a man actually got out of his car and came up and started looking inside my car. Then the light changed, and people started honking and yelling at him. I lost him after that. I feel like such a fugitive." She exhaled. "Did Collin get his pills?"

"Yes."

"Thank you."

Elizabeth walked in. "Mom, can I watch TV?"

"No, honey. Collin's sleeping."

"She can watch in my room," I said.

"You've got a room?" Addison asked.

"It's right through that door. I plan on watching over you."

Addison smiled. "You're my hero."

I took Elizabeth to my suite and turned on the television for her. By the time she was settled, Addison had finished putting away the food and was seated at the kitchen table waiting for me.

"I was going to tell you, my ex turned up this morning."

I sat down next to her. "Coincidence?"

"Yeah, right. He's got this scheme to make himself 'richer than God.' Or at least richer than Warren Buffett."

"And it involves Collin?"

"Of course. What worries me is that I can't stop Steve from seeing him. He still has visitation rights."

"But he knows that healing people makes Collin sick, doesn't he?"

"I told him, but remember, this is a man who said he couldn't come to the hospital and see Collin because his new wife was suffering stress over an upcoming photo shoot. He'll rationalize it somehow."

I cocked my head. "How does a smart woman like you fall for a guy like that?"

"Steve was charming."

"Yeah, sounds like it."

"No, really, he was. He was amazingly sweet. Everyone was always telling me how lucky I was to get him. And I believed them. He charmed everyone except my father. Dad saw through him. He kept asking me if I was sure about marrying him. The truth is, I think I was afraid that no one else would want me."

"No one would want you?"

She smiled at me. "I know you think I'm beautiful. You're very sweet that way. But I was definitely a late bloomer. I was a flat-chested kid with braces and acne. I was never asked out to the prom."

"That's still hard for me to believe."

"Oh, I could show you photos." She smiled shyly. "But thank you."

"When did you suspect there were snakes in Eden?"

"It was on our wedding day. I saw this other side of him. It was something stupid. I got a pimple on my cheek. Of course I was freaked out and I put a pound of makeup over it. I told Steve about it, thinking he'd make me feel better—you know, 'it's no big deal', or 'you can't see a thing.' Instead, he got mad at me. It didn't take long to learn that life for Steve is about appearances.

"I think that's why he's so distant from our son. Collin had nothing to offer Steve. Steve didn't want a good little boy; he wanted a little boy who was good at something. Someone who would make *him* look good. Collin could never be that Little League hero. Steve was really tough on him." Her eyes grew moist. "What hurt me the most is that Collin *tried*. He would try to do things that would make his father proud. He would draw pictures and make things with clay. He really wanted to please his dad. He never could."

"Until now," I said.

"Until now. Now he's freaking Babe Ruth," she said, shaking her head. "About a month after Steve left, a friend gave me a book about sociopaths. One of the case studies I read fit Steve to a T. I mean, dead on. They could have just changed names."

"I've met more than my share of sociopaths," I said. "They're very good at being charming, until you don't give them what they want. Then it's Ted Bundy. I was doing an interrogation with this guy—a certified sociopath, if I ever saw one—and he just got up in the middle of our Q and A and started to walk out."

"You let him?"

"Oh no. I had him on the ground before he made the hall. The cop handcuffed him and dragged him away, which was a shame because I was really sick of the guy and I was hoping he'd take a swing at me. There's a lot more of them out there than anyone realizes."

"So I made a mistake and fell for one. The question I have is, why do we have to keep paying for the same mistakes over and over? And why do our children have to pay for our mistakes?"

That was something I'd wrestled with my whole life.

"I forgot to tell you, Collin threw up a few minutes after we left the house."

She dropped her head in her hands. "If only he could heal himself," she said softly. She looked back up at me. "How are you doing? You looked really stressed."

I considered telling her about Collin and Tommy, but decided to wait. "I'm just tired. I only got a few hours sleep last night."

"No help from me. I'm sorry to drag you in to all this."

"Don't be."

"Would you like a backrub?"

I think it took some courage for her to ask this. "Yeah. I think I would."

"We'll use your room." She took my hand and led me past Elizabeth to the master bedroom in my suite. "Lizzy, I'm going to give Mr. Hurst a massage, so no disturbing us unless it's an emergency."

"Okay, Mom."

Once in the room, Addison helped me take off my shirt. Then I lay down on the bed. She kneeled on the bed next to me and began kneading my back muscles, moving up to my neck.

"I should give you one," I said. "You're the one with stress."

"This is how I deal with stress. I believe the best way to heal yourself is to help heal others."

"Unless you're Collin," I said. Addison's touch softened. I turned over to look at her and saw the hurt in her eyes. "I'm sorry." I pulled her on to me and held her. I fell asleep with her in my arms.

CHAPTER

Thirty

Earl just keeps on going, and going, and going . . .

✦NATHAN HURST'S JOURNAL✦

When I woke, I was alone in the suite. I pulled on my shirt and went to the door that separated Addison's suite from mine. I rapped once, then opened the door. Addison was at the kitchen counter slicing cheese.

"How was your nap?"

I yawned. "Good. How long was I out?"

"Almost four hours."

"Yikes."

"You needed the rest. Miche called about a half hour ago just to check up on you. I hope you don't mind that I answered your phone."

"I don't mind." I yawned again. "I'm going to run to the gym, then back to my place to get a few things. And I need to feed Earl."

"Who's Earl?"

"He's my fish."

She smiled. "I was just about to make grilled cheese sandwiches and tomato soup. Should I save you some?"

"No, I might be a while. I'll just grab something on the way."

✦

It felt good to get back in the gym. I worked out for a couple of hours, mostly just lifting weights, then picked up a hamburger on the way back to my apartment. When I got home I showered and shaved, then packed a bag with clothes and some grooming supplies. This time I remembered my coat. On my way out I dropped a pinch of fish food in the aquarium. I returned to the hotel around nine. The kids were already asleep. Addison was sitting on the couch, knitting. "Everything well at home?"

"Same as always."

"And Earl?"

"Earl's good."

"What kind of fish is Earl?"

"I don't know. Orange. He cost three dollars."

"Who takes care of Earl when you travel?"

"No one. Earl won't die. The rest of my fish died. I had a twenty-five-dollar Angel fish. He died. But Earl won't. I'm waiting for him to die so I can get rid of the aquarium. I haven't the heart to flush him."

She laughed at me. "Who names a fish Earl?"

"It's from that Dixie Chicks song, 'Goodbye Earl.' But Earl won't die. He'll never die. We'll be long gone and that fish will just keep on swimming. He's like an aquatic Energizer Bunny."

"You're cruel."

"Tell me about it."

Addison set down her knitting. "Let's go outside and talk," she said. She put on her coat, and we went outside and sat on the stairway just outside the room. She left the door slightly ajar so she could hear the kids if they woke. The air was sweet and moist, a portent of the coming storm. Addison looked up at the sky. "I like it when the air's like this. How many inches are they forecasting?"

"I think Eubank said six to eight inches in the valley. That should take care of Collin's fans."

"I hope so." She leaned her head on my shoulder, and for a moment she was quiet. I put my arm around her.

"I think I'm going to have to take Collin in. He's not getting much better. I keep having this horrible feeling that something bad is going to happen to him."

She looked at me. "You don't think anything's going to happen to him, do you?"

I hated the question. "Everything will turn out the way it's supposed to," I said.

"That's not very comforting."

I pulled her in tighter.

"Remember when you asked me when it was that I first found out that Collin could heal? I didn't tell you the complete truth." She rubbed her hand across my knee. "I was the first person he healed. A couple years before Collin's heart surgery, I came down with lupus. They didn't diagnose it for a while. I was tired all the time and at first they thought I had mono, then Epstein-Barr or chronic fatigue syndrome. Steve used to yell at me a lot. He said that the only problem with me was that I was lazy. Then I got this big, ugly rash on my face—a butterfly rash. That's when my doctor finally figured out what it was. When I told Steve about the diagnosis, he asked me if it was terminal." She looked down. "The way he asked . . . Can you imagine how much it hurts to know your spouse is hoping you'll die? I found out later that he'd already been having an affair. He left me a few months later."

"A few weeks after Collin's operation, I was in his room putting him to bed. I was tickling his back when he turned around and touched me on the face. This tremendous surge of energy went through me. You've felt it, so you know what a powerful thing it is. I had no idea what had happened; I thought I was having a hot flash or something. But the next day the rash and swelling were gone and I felt like myself again."

"That's really great."

"I thought so at first. But the next morning, Collin was so sick he couldn't get out of bed. It was less than a month later that we found out he had leukemia. I think his healing me and him getting cancer might be related."

"You don't know that."

"No. Not for sure. But what if they are?"

"I think Collin made a choice. And if he had the choice again, he'd heal you again." She took my arm and leaned into me, and we sat there in silence. Ten minutes later, the snow began to fall.

C H A P T E R

Thirty-One

Our thoughts are not arrows haphazardly shot out into the cosmos. They are boomerangs.

✦ NATHAN HURST'S JOURNAL ✦

Early Sunday morning, the snowplows were out in force. The grumbling of their blades woke me before sunrise, and I lay in bed looking at the ceiling. Then I parted the curtain for a stellar view of the hotel's back lot and a nearby Target store. There looked to be more than a foot of snow on the ground. I grabbed a book, the latest thriller by David Baldacci, and lay back on my bed to read. Around seven I could hear the sound of the television coming from Addison's room, so I pulled on my clothes and then softly knocked on the inside door that connected our two suites. Addison opened it. Her hair was mussed and she was wearing an ankle-length terrycloth robe.

"You're just in time for coffee," she said.

I stepped inside. Elizabeth sat cross-legged in front of the television, engrossed in a Bugs Bunny cartoon. I sat down at the kitchen table.

"Is Collin still asleep?"

"Yes. He tossed and turned all night. I'm exhausted. I've got sugar, Sweet'N Low, and Coffee-mate."

"Two Sweet'N Lows."

She poured the packages into my cup and brought it over to me. "So, what are your plans today?"

"I thought I'd drive by your house and see what's going on." I took a sip of coffee. "Miche said she'd watch the kids tonight if you'd like to go out for dinner. We'll keep our cell phones on this time," I quickly added.

"I would love to get out."

She finished stirring the creamer into her coffee. Then she came over and sat sideways across my lap. I wrapped my arms around her waist, and we kissed.

"That's gross," Elizabeth said.

"Get used to it, baby," Addison said. She looked me in the eyes. "You too."

We kissed again. When we parted, she said, "It's a little funny, isn't it? We're right back where we started, snowed-in at a hotel."

"Considering the company, not a bad fate," I said.

She smiled. "No, not a bad fate at all."

CHAPTER

Thirty-Two

In the Bible is a story of a pool called Bethesda
where the sick went to be healed.

"For an angel went down at a certain season into the pool,
and troubled the water; so that whoever then first
after the troubling of the water stepped in was made whole
of whatsoever disease he had."

In a way that story has repeated itself in Collin.

✦.NATHAN HURST'S JOURNAL.✦

I erroneously believed that the night's storm would blow away all the desperate folk at Addison's house. I couldn't have been more wrong. If anything, it galvanized the faithful. The road was lined with motor homes and trailers, most of them with out-of-state license plates.

As I neared Addison's home, I was amazed. The police tape was still intact, but just behind it were two dozen or more people, their arms raised toward the house, presumably absorbing the healing power emanating from it. There were people selling candles and prayer beads. One man was selling prayer cards with a picture of Collin that looked like it was snipped from a school group photo.

I pulled partially into the driveway, and an officer immediately moved to intercept me. It was Captain Johnson. I waved to him, and he recognized me. He walked to my window. "Can you believe this? We thought they'd be gone by now. It's a carnival."

"Everything but the corn dogs and the bearded lady," I said.

"No, we've got that too," Johnson replied. "Around noon a catering truck comes around with corndogs and junk. And I think I saw a bearded lady this morning. That, or the ugliest man I've ever seen."

I grinned. "Any excitement?"

"Last night there was some chanting that got the neighbors riled up. Then, about one in the morning, someone broke into the basement. We had to cuff him and drag him out. I guess there's some decked-out room down there. He kept shouting to everyone that there's a temple in the basement."

"It's her massage room," I said. "She's a massage therapist."

"I don't think she'll have any trouble getting clients after this. Other than that, it's been pretty peaceful. You know what's really crazy? Some doctors have filed complaints with the A.G.'s office that the boy's practicing medicine without a license."

"What are they going to do, sue him?" I said.

"I'm sure someone will. God bless America, land of the lawsuit."

I shook my head. "Addison left some of Collin's medication here. Can I go inside?"

"Yeah, just tell McClowsky we talked."

"Thanks."

There was an officer sitting on the couch inside the house reading one of Addison's *Cosmo* magazines. He looked up as I entered.

"Officer McClowsky? Johnson let me in," I said.

"No problem."

I found the pills in the medicine cabinet in Addison's bathroom, then I stopped to water her plants in the kitchen window above the sink. I walked back out to my car. As I was getting in, I noticed a man on the edge of the property standing in front of a large cardboard box. The words AUTHENTIC HEALING ARTIFACTS were written across it in black marker. I walked over to him. "So, what have you got here?"

"I'm selling some of the kid's personal effects. They've got powers."

"Really? Where'd you get them?"

"I'm a friend of the family."

"Is that right?"

"Sure, Allison and I go way back."

"Allison?"

"That's the mother's name. I always knew that kid was special. Once I bought a baseball cap of his at a yard sale and gave it to my nephew who has autism and now it's gone."

"The hat?"

"The autism. Doctor said it was a miracle. He said, 'Thirty years in practice and I ain't never seen anything like it.' Last night I sold a pair of socks to a man who put them on his hands for his arthritis. He came by this morning and told me he already felt better."

"How much did you get for the socks?"

"Hundred bucks. Fixed him right up."

"That's amazing."

"Sure is, it has healing properties. And I got stuff that's even more potent. Just take a look."

"No, I meant that you got some fool to pay you a hundred bucks for someone's used socks." I reached into the cardboard box and pulled out a T-shirt.

"Hey, I didn't say you could touch. I don't want this stuff to lose any of its virtue."

The shirt was clearly too large for Collin. I dropped it back in the box. "So, what happens when you sell out?"

"I got a whole truckload of his stuff back in my garage."

I grinned. "I bet you do."

CHAPTER

Thirty-Three

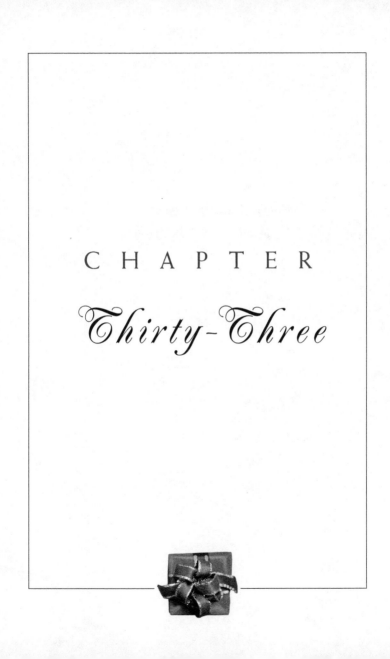

Small kindnesses often, unintentionally,
produce the biggest payoffs.

✴.NATHAN HURST'S JOURNAL.✴

Addison was upset by my report that the crowd outside her house had grown. The prospect of life returning to normal was rapidly diminishing. I was glad that we had planned to go out; she needed a break.

Miche arrived at the hotel a half hour early, excited to spend time with Collin and Elizabeth. On the way over, she had dropped by a friend's and filled up a backpack with children's movies. She was pleased to see us together again.

"Okay, Miche," I said, "we're going to dinner. You can reach me on my cell. I'll have it on the whole time."

"Don't worry, everything will be fine. Just have a good time."

Miche made the kids macaroni and cheese for dinner. When they were finished eating, she sent them off to the bedroom to watch TV while she threw a package of popcorn into the microwave and washed the dishes. When she finished, she joined the children in the bedroom.

"Here's the popcorn," Miche said. "Try not to spill it."

"What if I do?" Elizabeth asked.

"Then you'll help me clean it up."

"Do you have any kids?" Collin asked.

"No."

Elizabeth looked her over. "Aren't you old enough?"

"Thank you, Elizabeth," she said. "You get extra popcorn for that. Actually, my husband and I wanted to have kids, but the doctor said we can't have any."

"How come?" Collin asked.

"My body doesn't work right."

"It's broken?" Elizabeth asked.

"Yeah. It's broken."

"That's too bad," Elizabeth said. "You'd be a good mommy."

"Thank you, sweetie. But it's okay. We're going to adopt. There are lots of kids in this world who need parents, so maybe that's what God wants us to do."

Collin looked at her quizzically. "So God made it so you couldn't have children?"

"No. I think sometimes things just are what they are." She forced a smile, eager to change the subject. "All righty then, let's see what we've got." She dug through a backpack of DVDs and video games. "*Sponge Bob, Tom and Jerry, Aladdin, Scooby Doo*, and here's an oldie but goodie, *The Shaggy Dog*."

"*Scooby Doo*," Collin said.

"One vote for *Scooby Doo*. Elizabeth?"

"*Scooby Doo*," she said.

"*Scooby Doo* it is."

Miche put the DVD into the player and sat back on the bed, propped up by sofa cushions. Elizabeth sat on Miche's lap and asked her to braid her hair. Then Collin asked if she would tickle his back.

By the time the movie was over both Collin and Elizabeth

were asleep. Miche carried Elizabeth out to the front room and tucked her into the sofa bed. Then she went back into the master. Collin had wakened.

"You okay, buddy?"

"Yeah."

"You fell asleep." Miche pulled the sheets up to his neck. Then she switched off all the lights except a single floor lamp. "Is that too bright?"

"No. I like the light on. When is my mom coming back?"

"Soon. But I'll be here until then."

"Miss Miche?"

"Yes."

"You're really nice."

"Thanks, Collin. I think you are too."

"Can I give you a hug?"

Miche smiled. "Thank you. I'd like that."

She leaned over the bed and Collin put his arms around her. Miche felt something beautiful move through her, and for reasons she couldn't explain she started crying. "You really are a special little boy, aren't you?"

He didn't speak, but fell into his pillow and closed his eyes. Miche kissed his forehead. "Goodnight, little guy."

CHAPTER

Thirty-Four

"We're all moons. Some are just better at hiding their dark sides."

✦ NATHAN HURST'S JOURNAL ✦

Addison and I ate dinner at a basement Italian restaurant called Michelangelo's. It was authentic Italian—the employees were pretty much all green card–carrying immigrants from Lucca. Our server explained to us, without apology, that their small kitchen had only one stove with four burners, so the two of us would have to order the same meal. We agreed upon pumpkin ravioli with saffron sauce.

After we had finished eating, we drove up the mountain to look over the valley. The sky was clear with a few wisps of cloud streaking across it like spilt milk. Addison reached over and took my hand.

"Do you know how beautiful I think you are?" she said.

"You're deluded."

She frowned. "Every time I say how wonderful you are, you say something negative."

"You don't know the real me."

"Really? So, you're not the man with bronchitis who offered a complete stranger his room? Or the man who ran to my family's rescue after I thoughtlessly pushed him out of my life? Or the man who treats me like gold—that's not you either?"

I looked down.

"Nathan, everyone carries secrets. And everyone thinks no one would love them if they knew the person behind the mask. You're no exception. But I've seen the real you. I just wish that you could." She softly rubbed her hand over mine. "It has to do with what you saw during the massage, doesn't it? Your brother."

If I still had Tourette's, I probably would have been ticking like a wind-up monkey. I didn't look at her, but nodded.

"You couldn't tell me anything that would diminish my love for you," she said. I suppose I didn't believe her. But in all deceptions, there comes a time when concealment becomes more painful than truth. I was tired of carrying my secret, waiting for it to explode. I looked down at the steering wheel. "I've never told anyone this before."

"Then we'll hold each other's secrets."

It was a full minute before I spoke.

"I killed my brother."

I looked over at her, expecting to see horror on her face. Instead, she seemed thoughtful. At any rate, she clearly wasn't running for the door.

"Tell me about it."

"I was only eight. My brother, Tommy, was twelve. It was Christmas Day. My father gave Tommy a .22 rifle. My father believed every man should have a gun, that it was like a rite of passage. My mother was vehemently against it, but my father went ahead and bought it anyway.

"Tommy and I were pretending that we were hunters." I

hesitated. "I don't even remember pulling the trigger. There was just this explosion. Then there was blood everywhere. My brother never stopped looking at me. Even after he was gone, his eyes were open and he was staring at me. That's what I saw when you gave me the massage. I saw his eyes."

Addison put her arms around me and pulled my head against her breast and held me.

I could hear her heart as she rocked me with the gentle rise and fall of her chest. I suppose it was something I'd wanted to feel for almost twenty years. At that moment, I wanted to melt into this beautiful woman. She ran her fingers through my hair, then kissed my head.

"You've carried this guilt for all these years?"

"My mother blamed me for killing Tommy. She blamed my father for buying the gun. My father said it was his fault. I thought it was mine. When the next Christmas came around, my father killed himself with the gun he bought my brother."

"I'm so sorry."

"My mother never forgave me, for either death, and I've never forgiven myself. And then yesterday . . ." I moved my head up to look into her eyes. "Yesterday Collin saw Tommy. He talked to me."

For a moment she was speechless. "What did he say?"

"He told me to stop being sorry. And that the way to freedom was by freeing my mother." I swallowed. "I need to see her. Will you be okay if I leave for a while?' "

"Of course."

"I thought maybe I'd go tomorrow, after work."

She rubbed her hand across the back of my neck, then pulled me back into her.

"It's so liberating to tell you who I really am. I never would have believed that you could still love me."

Addison kissed my forehead. "I love you more because I know you better. I want you to see what's so obvious to me. How beautiful you are."

I closed my eyes and released myself to the warmth of her love.

CHAPTER

Thirty-Five

Love, like forgiveness, is often found in the confession of it.

✦ NATHAN HURST'S JOURNAL ✦

Addison and I returned to the hotel a little before midnight. Miche was sitting on the couch, reading a novel.

"How were they?" Addison asked.

"They were great. You have cute kids."

"Thanks for watching them."

"My pleasure. And I didn't have to be home listening to my husband and his friends compete for world domination. Double win." Miche turned to me. "Will you be coming in tomorrow?"

"I plan on it. How's Stayner?"

"Paranoid. He asked me twice today what you're sick with."

"So, everything's normal. I'll walk you out."

I took her arm as we crossed the icy parking lot to her car.

"So, what is she going to do?" Miche asked.

"I'm not sure. But I have a feeling that everything's moving toward some kind of resolution."

"Is that a good or bad thing?"

"Let's hope for good."

We stopped at her car. "So, are you in love?" Miche asked.

"Yes."

"I can tell. You have a different energy about you."

I opened her car door. "Give me your scraper and I'll do your windows."

She climbed inside her car and handed me a plastic scraper. She ran the engine and heater while I cleared the ice from her windows. When I was done, I opened her back door and threw the scraper inside. "See you tomorrow."

"She's lucky to have you, you know."

I just smiled at her, "Good night, Miche."

"Night, boss."

CHAPTER

Thirty-Six

Stayner fired me. Or maybe he just pushed me to the edge of the cliff and I chose to jump.

When I woke the next morning, the only one up was Elizabeth. She was sitting at the kitchen table reading a box of Cap'n Crunch cereal. Our conversation went like this:

"Good morning, Mr. Hurst."

"Good morning, Elizabeth."

"How did you sleep?"

"I slept well, thank you. And how did you sleep?"

"I slept well, thank you. Collin and Mommy are still asleep. Can you take me sleigh riding?"

"Actually, I need to go to work today."

"Then, can you make me cinnamon toast?"

"I think I can do that."

"Lots of cinnamon, please."

It took me three attempts to get the toast the correct shade, and I was fifteen minutes late leaving for work. Miche called me on my way in. "Warning: Stayner is on a rant. He says he wants to see you the second—not the minute, but the second—you get in."

"Thanks for the heads-up."

"Got your back."

I wondered what had gotten him so fired up. Yes, I'd missed

Louisville, but we had followed up with the store manager and orchestrated an arrest. Besides, in four years this was my first stumble. I parked my car and hurried up into the office.

Miche made a face when she saw me. "Good luck," she said gravely.

"Do I need it?"

I walked down the hall to Stayner's office. Martsie smiled at me, but there was something unpleasant in it.

"Larry in?"

"Yes. He'll be just a minute."

I sat down outside his office and picked up a copy of the MusicWorld magazine. Before I could settle on an article, Martsie's phone rang. "Yes, sir." She hung up. The pretense of a smile was gone, and suddenly I felt like an accused man before a frowning jury. "Mr. Stayner will see you now."

Stayner was clearly in bad humor. He started in on me before I could take a seat.

"Where have you been?"

"I'm sorry. I've had some personal issues come up."

"Well, I have a few issues myself with your performance of late. Two weeks ago you let a thieving employee off the hook in Philadelphia. You blow off an arrest in Louisville and then miss a week of work during our busiest season. Now I hear that you're using your assistant like your personal valet. And all you can say is, 'I've got some personal issues'? He looked over his glasses at me. "This isn't acceptable. I'm going to have to let you go."

"Are you joking?"

"Do I look like I'm joking?"

Now I was angry. "You know I've worked hundreds of hours without overtime and even with my 'performance of late,' my product return rate is still the highest in the office. And now that I take a little time off you're firing me?"

"Where have you been?"

"I've had some personal issues I've needed to take care of."

"I hear that you've been taking care of that boy in the news. Is it true?"

"Yes. I've been helping his mother."

"I meant, can he really heal?"

I tried to discern where the question was coming from. "Why?"

"Tell you what, I'll make you a deal. You bring him by the office and we'll see about letting you keep your job."

"Bring him by, or bring him by to fix your back?"

He didn't answer immediately. I wondered how he thought I wouldn't catch that. "As long as he's here."

"It doesn't work that way. He's very sick. Every time he heals someone, he gets sicker."

"Then I guess you have a problem."

I walked to the door and turned back. "You want me to endanger a little boy to keep my job? I'm not the one with a problem."

✦

I was glad that Miche was gone from her desk when I returned to my office; I was in no mood to debrief her on the encounter. I immediately began cleaning out my drawers into a cardboard file box. About five minutes into packing Miche walked in. "What are you doing?"

"I quit."

"Quit what?"

"My job."

She walked over to me, pulling away the box. "You can't quit me. We're a team."

"Stayner gave me an ultimatum. Collin fixes his back or he fires me. So I quit."

Miche's face reddened. "That creep. I'm going to—"

"You're going to do nothing. There's no reason for you to lose your job."

"You can't leave."

"I don't have a choice."

"This isn't right. This company owes you." Then her voice softened. "*I* don't want you to leave."

I walked over and hugged her. "You're the best thing that's happened to me since I got here. This doesn't change that. And if I ever get married, you're still going to be my best-maid, or whatever you'd call it."

Her sadness was overcome by anger.

"This isn't over," she said. "I'm going to get your job back."

"And how are you going to do that?"

"I have leverage."

"Leverage," I said, nodding. "May I please have my box back?" Miche relinquished her hold on the box, and I began filling it again. "I'm going up to Pocatello to see my mother. I'll call you when I get back."

"If I fix things, will you stay?"

"What do you mean?"

"If I get Stayner to apologize for being such a creep and offer you your job back, will you stay?" Her loyalty was endearing if naïve.

I stopped putting things in the box. "You get Stayner to ask me back, I'll stay."

"I'm holding you to that," Miche said and walked out of my office.

CHAPTER

Thirty-Seven

Fear has led to more retribution than justice ever will.

✦NATHAN HURST'S JOURNAL✦

Even my detailed description of the melee from the day before couldn't have prepared Addison for what she saw as she drove down her street. The crowd around her home had grown still larger. There was a patrol car in her driveway parked backward to the street. An officer got out and pulled back the tape so Addison could enter.

There was a new addition to the crowd from the day before—a burgeoning group of paparazzi. Several photographers and videographers rushed her car as she pulled into her driveway. Addison opened the garage door by remote and drove directly in; she didn't get out of her car until the door had closed behind her. As she walked into her kitchen, a police officer met her.

"Officer Robertson," he said, introducing himself.

Addison recognized him from the first day of the seige. "Thanks for watching over my place."

He grinned. "Ain't this something? You can tell it's Christmas from all the fruitcakes outside." He laughed at himself. "I thought they'd be gone by now. But they just keep on coming."

"Can't you just make them go?" she asked.

"They have a constitutional right to peaceable assembly. As long as they don't trespass or constitute a clear and present danger, there's not a thing we can do."

"Don't I have a right to privacy?"

"You've become a public figure. People stand outside movie stars' homes all the time, selling souvenirs, maps, bobble-head dolls. The whole shebang."

She sat down on the couch and rubbed her temples. "We just want our lives back."

"I was going to tell you, your ex came by the house yesterday. He said he had a visitation with the children. I hope you don't mind, but I told him where you're staying."

Addison groaned.

Just then, one of the other police officers stepped inside the front door.

"Mrs. Park, there's a man here who says he's your pastor. Pastor Tim?"

"Oh, thank goodness. Let him in."

The officer opened the door wider. "You can come in, Pastor."

A gray haired, middle-aged man wearing a brown felt hat and a tweed overcoat stepped inside. He was carrying a gold fruitcake tin.

Officer Robertson grinned when he saw the tin. "I'll leave you two alone." He walked outside.

The man smiled at Addison. "Hello, Addy."

"Pastor Tim, I'm so glad you came. Your timing is perfect. I just stopped by the house to get some things."

"It's all God's timing, dear." He gave her a hug. "How are you doing?"

"We're surviving."

"Certainly better than the alternative." He handed Addison his gift. "Denise sent over her famous fruitcake. To her 'watching over the flock' means feeding it."

"Tell her thank you. Do you have time to sit?"

"I'd love to." He sat down on the couch. He removed his hat and lay it on his lap. Addison sat on the opposite end of the couch.

"Would you like something to drink?"

"No. I'm fine, thank you."

"I'm sorry we missed worship service last Sunday. We were kind of hiding out."

"No worries. Actually, it was probably for the best."

"Why is that?"

"You'd never believe how many calls I've received about your son."

"About Collin? Why?"

"Of course, most are from people who want to know how they can help. But a few of them are afraid."

Addison bristled. "That's ridiculous. Why would anyone be afraid of Collin?"

"Some of them are worried that his power comes from the devil."

"How could anyone believe that?"

"You'd be surprised, Addy. People are funny about the spiritual world. They're comfortable with miracles on paper but show them a burning bush today and they'd run for a fire extinguisher." Pastor Tim shook his head. "Frankly, it's not the ones who are afraid of Collin who worry me most."

Addison looked at him quizzically. "Then who?"

"How do I say this?" The Pastor's demeanor took on the gravity of a Sunday sermon. "Sometimes people forget that faith precedes the miracle. They say, 'give me fire and then I'll cut some firewood'. It's those people who are always looking for a sign without reason or faith attached. Collin's that kind of miracle. There are people, in our very own congregation, who would worship your son."

"Worship Collin? But he's just a little boy."

"So was Jesus, once." He clasped his hands together. "If what I've read is true, Collin has a very powerful gift—one of the very gifts Jesus had. That's an enormous responsibility, especially for a little boy. There's a reason that Jesus always admonished those he healed to tell no one; he didn't want people following him for the wrong reason. He knew that human nature was such that people would follow him just to be healed, not because of his teachings or righteousness. The healing that God was most interested in was that of the spirit." He frowned. "I just worry about how they might treat your son."

"What are we supposed to do?"

"I wish I knew the answer. But for now it's probably best that you don't bring Collin to church for a little while. At least until things calm down."

"But he loves going to church."

"I know. He's a good boy. I just don't want something bad to happen to him."

"But what if things never calm down? What if it gets worse?"

He frowned. "I don't know. I guess we'll cross that bridge when we come to it."

Addison looked down.

"I'm sorry, Addy. I didn't mean to add to your burden. What can I do to help? Do you need a place to stay?"

"That's very sweet, Pastor, but we'll be okay. Thank you."

"Don't thank me, I didn't do anything except deliver some fruitcake. And most people wouldn't think that's a very friendly thing to do." The pastor stood. "I'll let you go. You have my cell phone number?"

"Yes."

"If you decide to come to church, I'll be there with you."

"I know you will."

Addison walked him to the door and hugged him. "Thanks for coming."

"Take care of yourself."

Addison shut the door and cried.

CHAPTER

Thirty-Eight

There is no greater paradox than "self-interest."

✦NATHAN HURST'S JOURNAL✦

Miche walked uninvited into Stayner's office. Stayner was on the phone and covered his mouthpiece. "Excuse me."

Miche held her ground.

He stared at her, amused by her insolence. "I'll have to call you back." He set the phone in its cradle. "So, Ms. Checketts, am I to understand that you plan on quitting with Mr. Hurst?"

"How dare you fire Nate? He's the best employee you have. He never takes breaks, and he catches more theft than anyone who's ever had that job. You're firing him because he won't compromise the child he's protecting. Corporate's going to hear about this."

"I'm firing him for malfeasance and misfeasance, both of which I've documented and submitted to HR. And I accept your resignation as well."

"You should know I'm filing a sexual harassment suit against you."

He shook his head cynically. "You're threatening me with that? Couldn't you have come up with something better?"

"I have corroboration for your behavior. Lots of it."

"Corroboration?" he said. "That's a big word for you, isn't it?"

Miche walked to the door and asked Martsie to come in.

Stayner glared at his assistant. "You should know I've just fired Ms. Checketts, and I'll fire anyone who is in on this mutiny with her. I'm giving you a chance to turn around and walk out."

Martsie crossed her arms. "Mr. Stayner, I can guarantee you that once HR learns about the weekend business trip you invited me on or the lingerie you bought me on Executive Assistant's day, *you're* the one who'll be looking for a job."

"This is calumny."

"Now *that's* a big word," Miche said.

"I've kept a journal, Larry," Martsie continued . . ." And so have other women here. There's a reason they've nicknamed you Hands. Collectively we've recorded more than forty harassment violations. You should also know I've kept a file of some very *special* e-mail I'm sure the company attorneys would be interested in. And so would your wife. All I have to do is push Send and the fireworks begin."

"Remember Quinn in acquisitions?" Miche asked. "And next to you he looked like a monk."

"This is extortion!"

"We *are* threatening you, aren't we?" Miche turned to Martsie. "I say we just file and let the chips fall where they may. I'm betting corporate gives Nate Larry's job anyway." She turned back to Stayner. "But either way, I'm sure *you're* gone. Good luck landing another executive position with this on your record."

Stayner stared at them, his expression a mixture of anger and fear. "What do you want?"

"First, the harassment stops completely," Miche said. "The minute you so much as bump into one of us, the deal's off. Second, you write Nate a letter of commendation. Third, you apologize to Nate and get him to take his job back with time off for exemplary behavior. And you better be convincing, because if he *doesn't* take his job back, there's no deal."

"I can't make him take his job back."

"Then let's hope you're very, very persuasive."

"How much time off?" Stayner asked.

"Until the New Year."

"We get Christmas off anyway," Martsie said.

"Right," Miche said. "Give him until January seventh."

He looked back and forth between the two women, his eyes eventually settling on Martsie. "I can't believe you'd do this."

"I won't lie to your wife anymore, Larry. And those Wednesday racquetball games aren't fooling anyone. Everyone knows about Cheryl in accounting."

"So what will it be?" Miche asked. "It's your choice."

Stayner settled back in his chair. "I believe you ladies already made it for me."

CHAPTER

Thirty-Nine

*Forgiveness does not require us to close our eyes
but rather to truly open them.*

✦ NATHAN HURST'S JOURNAL ✦

Everything about the drive to Pocatello felt different this time. Just two weeks earlier on the same highway I had lamented the sameness of my life. I suppose I had tempted fate. Now, as I headed back to Idaho, everything in my life was in commotion. Not the least of which was my career. There was something both frightening and hopeful about it all. Most peculiar about the drive was my suspicion that I wasn't alone. I kept wondering if Tommy was sitting in the passenger seat next to me. I let him know that if he were, I was glad for his company. I was going to need his help; I wasn't sure if I would be able to do what I needed to do when the time came. *If* it came. My mother had been mentally absent for years. What if I were too late?

I found my mother parked in her wheelchair in the multipurpose room, along with a half dozen other residents, watching *Wheel of Fortune*. I crouched down next to her wheelchair.

"Mom, it's Nathan."

She continued to look ahead, fixated on the television. "Is there a *B*, Pat?" she said.

"Mom, I need to talk to you."

She looked at me blankly. "Where have you been, Tommy?"

"I'm taking you to your room so we can talk." I took the chair by its handles and began to push when she let out a piercing, high-pitched wail.

"Okay," I said. "We'll wait."

"Shut up over there," a man said. "I can't hear Sajack."

I sat down on the arm of a vinyl chair next to her. "I'd like to spin," my mother said.

It was more amusing watching the residents than the show; they were much more passionate than the onscreen contestants. One of the men kept saying, "Turn those letters, Vanna Va-Room," and "What happened to Chuck Woolery?" Another woman said, "That Vanna's just so lovely" every time a letter was turned. When the show was nearly over, a nurse came in for my mother. "Candace, it's time for your blood pressure medicine."

She put the pill in my mother's mouth and guided a small Dixie Cup of water to her lips. My mother choked a little on it. "Good job, Candace," she said then left the room. Almost immediately after her departure, one of the spryer residents confiscated the television remote and turned the channel to *Baywatch*. There was a loud outcry, and I took advantage of the diversion to get my mother out of the room.

I pushed her down the tile corridor scanning the brass room numbers nailed to the doors until I came to my mother's bedroom. It was a box of a room with oak furniture that looked as worn down as the residents. Another woman, I assume my mother's roommate, was inside and snoring loudly. I pulled the cloth curtain that hung from a track on the ceiling, partitioning the room. Then I sat on the edge of my mother's bed. She seemed only remotely aware of the change of scenery.

"Mom, it's me, Nathan."

It was nearly a minute before she said, "Where's Tommy?"

I leaned forward, looking my mother in the eyes. "Mom, Tommy is dead."

She showed no expression.

"Tommy is dead," I repeated. "Do you understand? Tommy's been dead for twenty years."

My mother didn't move except for grinding her dentures.

"On Christmas day Tommy and I were playing with his new gun and it went off. You blamed Dad and me for what happened. But I think most of all you blamed yourself. I think you also blame yourself for Dad taking his life. But Dad made a choice—and that was his choice, not yours. It's time for all the blame to stop." I put my face against hers. "Mom, Tommy came to me. He told me it's time to stop being sorry."

I looked in her face, but she showed no expression. Maybe it *was* too late. Maybe this exercise was meant just for me. If that were the case, then there were still things that needed to be said.

"Do you know how many times I wanted to hear you say that you still loved me. I grew up hating you for withholding that from me. But I'm tired, Mom. I'm tired of holding onto that resentment. I want you to know that I forgive you. And I hope you can forgive me too."

She looked down at the floor. "I'd like to buy a vowel," she said.

"It's okay, Mom. It's okay." I put my arm around my mother and lay my head against her shoulder. "I'm sorry, Mom. For everything we lost. Even if it is too late."

Her lips moved, but their movement was without voice. Her eyes moved to mine. Then she mumbled something.

"Did you say something, Mom?"

I put my ear to her mouth, feeling her lips against my face for the first time since I was a little boy. Then I heard it. Slow and distorted, but still understandable.

"I'm sorry, Natie."

CHAPTER

Forty

All miracles are an expression of love.
A Course in Miracles

✦ NATHAN HURST'S JOURNAL ✦

Addison was brushing her teeth when she heard a knock. She rinsed out her mouth, then walked to the front room and opened the door. Steve stood in the threshold.

"Morning, Addy."

"What are you doing here?"

"I came to visit my children."

Addison looked over and saw Franzen standing behind him, carrying an oxygen tank.

"Oh no. He's not coming in here."

Steve turned back and smiled confidently at Franzen. "We'll be just a minute." He stepped into the suite, forcing Addison aside. "Be cool, Addy."

"You can't come in here." Steve grabbed her by the arm and pulled her back into the kitchen.

Addison struggled to free herself from his grip. "Let go of me."

"Not until you settle down."

"No, Steve, this is my room and that man can't come in here."

"Keep your voice down."

"No."

"You can't keep me from him. He's my son too."

"I'm not trying to keep him from you. But that man can't see him. Collin's really sick right now."

"You can't stop me, Addy."

"I'm going to call the police."

"The police told me where you were." He pushed her into the open pantry. "Now calm down."

"Stop it. You're hurting me."

He shoved her up against the shelves on the back wall. "I said keep it down."

"Don't, Steve. Please."

His face was tight and crimson. "Do you have any idea what this means? Three million dollars. That's a lot of heart transplants, baby. Where did you think that money was going to come from? But you don't think about that, do you? Just so long as you get that alimony."

"I don't care if it's a billion dollars."

"Of course you don't. You don't have to pay for anything. I do. Failure is not an option here. I've hung everything on this."

"Healing people draws life out of him. I'm not making this up, Steve. He's really sick. This could kill him."

"Unless it's someone *you* want to heal. You never answered me, Addy. What happened to your lupus? Are you afraid he might not have enough juice left for you? Are *you* killing our son?"

"I didn't ask him to heal me. I didn't know it would hurt him."

"You think I would hurt my own son?" Steve said.

"You already have."

Steve sneered. "You'd do anything to get back at me, wouldn't you? But you're not going to take this away from me."

"I'm telling you the truth."

He shoved her again, much harder this time, and she hit the side of her head against a shelf, cutting her ear. A stream of blood ran down her jaw. When she reached up to touch her ear, the door slammed on her. Steve propped a metal chair from the kitchen table under the doorknob. Addison pushed on the door, but couldn't move it. "Let me out of here. Steve, let me out."

"When we're done."

Steve walked out into the front room. Franzen had let himself in during the tussle and was sitting on the sofa. Franzen looked at him darkly. "Problems?"

Steve shook his head. "Ex-wives. Can't live with them. Can't kill them and feed their sorry carcasses to rats."

Franzen grinned. "I know the feeling."

"I think my son's back here." They both heard Addison pounding on the door. "That won't do," Steve said. He turned the front room television on loud enough to drown her out.

"You locked her in the closet?" Franzen asked.

"Seemed like the best place for her."

Franzen laughed. "That's the spirit."

Steve led Franzen to the bedroom and opened the door. The light was off, but the shades were partially open, illuminating the room with the winter sun. Collin lay in the bed. His eyes were open.

"Hey, buddy, it's me."

Collin looked over. "Dad?"

"Yeah. How are you?"

"Where have you been?"

"I've been traveling a lot. Didn't your mother tell you?"

"No."

"Well, I'm sure she meant to," Steve said. Collin glanced uneasily at the strange man standing in his room. "Collin, I want you to meet someone. This is Mr. Franzen. He's a friend of mine and he's really sick. I want you to make him better."

Collin's eyes darted back and forth between the two men. "Where's Mom?"

"She's in the kitchen. She'll be here in a minute. So go ahead and make him better."

"I need to ask Mom."

"You don't need to ask her. I'm your father and I'm telling you it's okay, so it's okay."

✦

"Collin!" Addison screamed. She backed up as far as possible and threw her body against the pantry door but without effect, except for a sharp pang that shot down her shoulder. "Collin! Don't touch that man! Don't touch him!"

✦

Collin couldn't hear his mother but he knew that something was wrong. The color around the two men was especially muddied and dark, and it frightened him. The gentleness of his father's voice didn't match what he saw. "Go on, son. It's okay."

The old man limped over to the bed, carrying the oxygen tank. "Hello, son. My name is Riley." He sat down on the edge of a chair near Collin's bed. "How old are you, son? Nine, ten?"

"I'm nine."

"That's a good age. I wish I were nine again. I have a grandson about your age. He plays a lot of baseball. Do you like baseball?"

"I can't run very good."

"That's okay. You can do something much, much better. Something much more special. Your father says you can make people better. Is that true?"

Collin didn't trust the question.

"Answer him," Steve said sharply.

Collin jumped, startled by his father's tone. "Yes, sir."

Franzen turned to Steve. "That's enough," he snapped. He turned back to Collin. "I'm sorry about that. It won't happen again." He suddenly smiled. "Christmas is coming. I bet you're getting pretty excited."

Collin looked at him dully.

"If you could have anything in this world, anything at all, an Xbox, a go-kart, a swimming pool in your backyard, if all you had to do was ask and you'd have it, what would you ask for?"

"I don't want anything," Collin said.

At first Franzen seemed vexed by Collin's response, then

he began to nod. "I think I see the problem here." The man's forehead furrowed with concern. "Let me ask you something. I'm sorry to ask you this, because kids shouldn't have to think about things like this. But does your mother ever worry about money?"

Collin nodded.

"Does she worry about money a lot? Like when there's a bill and she can't pay it."

Collin nodded again. "Sometimes when we want something and it costs too much."

"That's a bad feeling, isn't it? I know exactly how that feels. My mother used to worry too. It always made me feel bad inside. Sometimes it even made my stomach hurt. Does it make you feel bad inside?"

"Yes, sir."

"You know, Collin, it takes a lot of money to raise children. All that food and clothes and shoes and lessons. Of course, the most expensive thing of all is the medical stuff like doctors and hospitals and medicine. Believe me, they cost a lot of money. Did you know that?"

Collin shook his head, averting his eyes in shame. He had suspected as much, but his mother never said anything about it.

"I'm sure your mother wouldn't tell you something like that. She wouldn't want you to worry. Mothers are just that way, always looking out for you, aren't they?"

"Yes, sir."

"But I'm telling you, those doctors and hospitals, they really sock it to you. Did you know that one pill can cost more than a hundred dollars? It's not your fault, but I bet your mom really feels bad about that sometimes."

Collin felt a lump rise in his throat. He wanted to cry. Franzen looked at him sympathetically.

"Collin, I can tell that you're a good boy. I bet you love your mother a lot, don't you?"

"Yes, sir."

"You know what? I can help your mother. Let me tell you a little secret." He suddenly leaned in close, which made Collin feel even more uneasy. He didn't like the way the man smelled. "Collin, I'm a very rich man. I have a lot of money. And I can help your mother. You'd like that, wouldn't you?"

Collin nodded.

"But I can't do that if I'm really sick, can I? And if I die, well, then other people will just take my money. So do you want to help your mother?"

"Yes, sir."

"I thought so. I'm going to give you a chance. I'm just going to sit right here and let you make me better. Then I'll see to it that your mother is taken care of. I promise you. Does that sound okay?"

Collin nodded but otherwise didn't move.

"I don't even know how this works. You know more than I do. Do you need to touch me? Or is it like magic and you have to say special words, like Harry Potter?"

"I just touch."

"Does it matter where you touch?' "

"No."

"Okay. I'll sit right here so you can reach me." He leaned partially over the bed.

Collin looked at him and swallowed.

"You want to do this for your mother, don't you?"

"Yes, sir." Collin slowly reached out and touched Franzen on the shoulder. Franzen took a deep breath and closed his eyes. After a few seconds Collin removed his hand.

Steve looked at Franzen expectantly. "How do you feel?"

Franzen opened his eyes. "The same."

"Maybe it takes a while to take effect." He looked at Collin. "Does it take a while?"

Collin looked down.

"Does it?"

"No, sir."

"Did you heal him?"

Collin shook his head. "No."

"Collin, heal him. That's an order."

Collin began to cry. "I tried."

"Don't try. *Do it.*"

✦

Elizabeth was in the other suite watching television when she heard Addison's shouting through the bedroom wall. She walked in looking for her. "Mommy!" She walked into the kitchen. "Mommy!"

Addison pressed up against the door. "Elizabeth. It's Mommy. I'm in here. Open the door."

"Mommy?" The little girl got down on her hands and knees and looked through the crack in the pantry. She stuck her fingers under the door. "Why are you hiding in there?"

Addison crouched down and suddenly felt a little dizzy. Her ear throbbed with pain. "Lizzy, I can't get out. What's against the door?"

"A chair."

"Can you move it?"

Elizabeth stood up and pushed on it. "No."

Addison thought about how it was likely propped. "Lizzy, are the chair's front legs in the air?"

"Uh-huh."

"Grab the chair's front legs and lift them as hard and as high as you can."

"But the chair will fall."

"That's okay, honey. You won't get in trouble."

"Promise?"

"Promise. Lizzy, do it. Now!"

☀

In the room, Collin leaned forward and touched the man again. Franzen closed his eyes and braced himself. Again nothing happened.

"What's going on here?" Franzen scowled.

"What's going on, Collin?" Steve asked.

"I don't know," Collin said.

"You're doing this on purpose," Steve said, his voice rising.

"No, I'm not."

Just then Addison burst through the door. "Get away from my son." She ran to Collin's side, putting herself between him and Franzen, shoving Franzen back in the process.

Steve started toward her. "You're gonna pay for that."

"I've already called the police. They're on their way."

"What are you going to tell them?" Steve said smugly, "that I'm visiting my son?"

"I told them what you did. You're a lawyer, you know how many laws you broke. Battery. Unlawful imprisonment."

"I had nothing to do with this," Franzen said.

"You were an accomplice. They're going to arrest both of you."

Franzen grabbed his oxygen and began backing toward the door. His eyes locked with Steve's. "I'll be calling the partners on the way back." Then he turned to Collin. "You're a fraud."

"Get out," Addison said.

Steve blocked the doorway. "Mr. Franzen, this is just a hiccup. We can still make this work."

"Get out of my way." He pushed his way past Steve and stumbled out the door.

Steve spun toward Addison. "You poisoned him against me." He then pointed a finger at Collin. "I'm going to lose my job because of you."

Addison's eyes were fierce. "The police are on their way and I'm still bleeding. So unless you want to leave in handcuffs, do what you do best and run."

"I'll make sure you regret this," he said, then turned and left.

Collin fell into his mother. Addison wrapped her arms around him. "You okay?"

He began to cry, and she pulled him in close. "I'm sorry, Mom. I tried."

"You've nothing to be sorry about. You did everything right."

He suddenly pulled back and looked at his hand. It was red with blood. "What happened to your ear?"

"I hit it on a shelf."

"Did Daddy do that?"

Addison wanted to lie, but she knew it was pointless. "Yes."

Collin reached up and touched her ear. The bleeding and pain stopped immediately.

Addison rested her chin on Collin's head. "Oh, baby, please don't heal me anymore."

"I can't help it."

She held him. "You did the right thing. You shouldn't have healed that bad man."

"I tried, Mom. He said he would help you. But I couldn't."

"You couldn't?"

"No. I don't like him."

CHAPTER

Forty-One

Sometimes to move forward we must be willing to look back.

✦NATHAN HURST'S JOURNAL✦

I spent a few more minutes with my mother before I pushed her back to the multipurpose room. The *Baywatch* coup had been put down, and the residents were contently absorbed in *Jeopardy!*

Before I left her I told my mother that I would return in a couple weeks. I don't know if that even registered with her, but I hoped it would. As I walked out, I heard a woman say, "That Trebek's a fine-looking fellow."

As I drove from the nursing home's parking lot, I made a decision to visit my childhood home. I hadn't seen it since the day I moved out more than a decade earlier. At the time I swore that I'd never go back.

The house was only about three miles from the nursing home. I didn't recognize it at first. My mother had kept a perfectly manicured yard with impressive flowerbeds and well-groomed shrubs, and trees. Even when the garden was dormant in winter there was order to it. When I was six, she had been awarded the local tabloid's Green Thumb award. She got her picture in the paper and dinner for two at a local buffet. It was a proud moment for all of us.

In the center of the yard a hand-painted For Sale sign rose

from a snowbound clump of thistle. Weeds stuck up through the dirty snow.

Paint peeled from the house's wood siding, and its window screens, the old steel kind, were both rusted and torn. The only thing that looked vaguely the same was the sycamore in the front yard, where a few of the boards that Tommy had nailed in it—so we could climb—still remained.

I parked my car and began walking around the place, my hands deep in my pockets. Everything, with exception of the sycamore, was much smaller than I remembered. My palatial birthplace was a cracker box of a home. There are Eastside garages with more square footage. Things always seem so much bigger when you're a child. I think that's true of events as well as locale.

"Look what they've done to the place, Tommy," I said aloud.

Suddenly a plain-looking woman with lifeless eyes opened the front door. She hid behind the aluminum storm door as if it were a shield. "Can I help you?"

I stopped. "I'm sorry. I used to live here."

She looked at me suspiciously.

"You wouldn't consider letting me have a look inside, would you?"

"No."

"Of course. Do you mind if I look around a bit? For old times' sake."

She hid a little more behind the door. "I'd rather you didn't."

Like there's anything to steal. "My name is Nathan Hurst. I was born in this house. I'm back in town visiting my mother and thought I'd stop by."

"We've only been here three years." Her lips tightened as she pointed across the street. "The man in that blue house said someone was killed in this house. Said a boy shot his brother."

"How long has the house been up for sale?" I asked.

"Couple years."

"I wouldn't go sharing that little gem with your prospects. People tend to get a little squeamish about things like that. May help."

She just stared at me, unsure of how to respond.

"Ciao," I said. I'd seen enough. The woman disappeared behind the front door.

Back in my car, the first thing I did was call Addison. She didn't answer; I had no idea she was locked in a closet. I started my car and headed for home. I was near the Utah-Idaho border when I got a call from Stayner. I almost didn't take the call but my curiosity got the better of me. If I hadn't seen his name on the caller ID, I probably wouldn't have recognized his voice. "Hey, Nate, what's up?"

The only thing more bizarre than his question was his chummy tone.

"You fired me."

"Yeah. Well, I need to talk to you about that. That wasn't really me."

"It looked like you."

"No, it was the meds talking. And I had just got off the phone with the wife. You know how that makes me. The bottom line is, you're not fired. Never were. I didn't mean any of it. Everything you said was true. You are our best employee. You're the Tiger Woods of MusicWorld security."

"So you don't want me to bring Collin by?"

"No, of course not. I mean, it would be nice if he's around, but no, not if it's going to hurt him. I think it's great how you're taking care of that kid. In fact, I'd like to help somehow. So I'm giving you some time off. You've got until January seventh to relax and take care of things."

"With pay?"

"Absolutely."

"And this was your idea?"

"Who else's would it be?"

I didn't answer the question. "This is very generous of you."

"I'm a generous guy. I'll take that as a yes, and I'll see you on January seventh. Have an awesome Christmas and a happy New Year."

He hung up. I couldn't wait to find out how Miche had done it.

I called her immediately.

"So Hands called?" she said proudly.

"A new-and-improved Hands."

She laughed. "So, are you staying?"

"We had a deal."

"Excellent."

"But you have to tell me how you did it."

"No, that's *my* secret."

"You didn't bribe him, did you?"

"Heavens no. Threaten maybe, but not bribe. I told you I had leverage."

"Miche, thanks."

"I've got your back, boss."

✦

It was past nine when I got back to the hotel. I was surprised to find Elizabeth alone. She was lying on her stomach on the floor in the front room doing a puzzle. "Hi, Mr. Hurst."

"Where's your mom?"

"She's in your room crying."

Addison was curled up in the fetal position, sobbing, on the floor in my bedroom. I got down on my knees and put my arms around her.

"What happened?"

She spoke through sobs. "Steve came. He tried to make Collin heal someone."

"You've got blood on your blouse."

"He threw me against the shelves in the pantry."

I pulled her hair back to examine the wound but couldn't find one. "Where are you bleeding?"

"Collin healed me."

"Is Collin okay?"

"He's sleeping. He didn't heal the man."

"Where do I find Steve?"

"No, please, don't go after him. I already called the police." She snuggled into me. "Please don't leave me. I can't do this alone anymore."

I kissed her head. "I won't leave you. Ever. I promise."

CHAPTER

Forty-Two

I've heard it said we must be like children to enter Heaven.
Not until tonight did I understand.

✦NATHAN HURST'S JOURNAL✦

It was more than a half hour before Addison began to calm down. We were still lying on the floor when Elizabeth walked into the room. "Collin's breathing funny."

In the few seconds it took to get to the other suite, Collin had stopped breathing completely. Addison put her ear against his chest, then turned to me, her eyes wide with terror. "Call 911." She immediately began CPR.

By the time the paramedics arrived, Addison's efforts had produced a faint heartbeat. Addison climbed in the back of the ambulance with Collin. I drove behind them with Elizabeth, silently praying.

"Is Collin going to die?" Elizabeth asked. Her voice was pinched with fear.

"I don't know, honey." I kept wondering if this was the day his grandfather had prophesied.

When the ambulance reached Salt Lake Regional, Collin's skin had turned a pale blue. He had an IV in his neck, a catheter, an A-line bag, an oximeter, pads on his bare chest, an arm cuff, and a nasal gastric tube; it was difficult to see the little boy under all the apparatus.

They took Collin immediately up to the ICU. Elizabeth

and I joined Addison in the waiting room. I had called Miche from the car; even though she was already in bed, she arrived within the hour. Her face mirrored our concern. "How can I help?"

"Could you help look after Elizabeth?"

"Of course. Do you want me to take her home?"

Elizabeth was in the corner of the room looking at a Dr. Seuss book. Even though she was out of earshot I spoke softly. "Not yet. Just in case . . ." I didn't finish. "Maybe you could take her for a walk. Anything to keep her distracted."

"No problem." She walked to Elizabeth. "Hey, Lizzy. Want to go on a little walk?"

"Can we buy Collin a bear?"

"Let's see if we can find a bear store still open."

Miche took her hand, and they walked out of the room.

Addison didn't say a word; she just sat alone with her head down, praying. It was past midnight before we saw a doctor. She was a young Chinese-American woman. She wore surgical greens, her mask tied around her neck.

"Mrs. Park?"

Addison stood. "Yes?"

"I'm Doctor Berg. Your son is stable. We've got his oxygen up. We had to give him a blood transfusion; with his chemo treatments he didn't have enough red blood cells to carry enough oxygen."

"But he's okay now?"

"For the time being, but it's only temporary. Heart failure is imminent."

"What about a heart transplant?"

The doctor looked distressed. "Mrs. Park, your son's not a candidate for a transplant. He was removed from the recipient list."

"What?"

"Didn't your oncologist discuss this with you?"

Addison turned pale. "What are you going to do, just let him die?"

"Mrs. Park . . ."

"My son risked his life to heal others. And when he needs something, all you can tell me is he's not on the list?"

"I'm sorry. I know how you must feel."

"Have you lost a child?"

The doctor frowned. "No, but—"

"Then don't tell me you know how I feel."

"I'm very sorry, but this is something I have no power over. There are strict protocols that we have to follow." She took a deep breath. "I need to ask you if you would be willing to sign a DNR."

Addison began to cry.

"What's that?" I asked.

"It's a do-not-resuscitate order."

"What if she doesn't sign it?"

"Every time the child codes we'll perform heroic measures until they don't work anymore. It will only prolong his pain."

"I want to see my boy," Addison said.

The doctor looked at her. "I'll take you up. He's sedated. It will be a while before he's conscious."

None of us spoke as we rode the elevator up to the eighth floor and followed her into the ICU.

Collin was hooked up to machines that monitored a dozen different bodily functions. Addison walked to his side and touched him. "Collin." He didn't respond, and she put her hand over her eyes.

We sat in the room watching Collin sleep. Maybe an hour had passed when I went down to check on Miche. Elizabeth was asleep on her lap.

"How's it going?" Miche asked. There was hope in her voice.

"Not well. He needs a heart transplant. But they've dropped him from the list."

"Why would they do that?"

"It's because of his cancer."

"I'm so sorry."

"We're just waiting for him to wake up."

"What do you want me to do?"

"Could you stay a little longer? It might be Lizzy's only chance to talk to him."

Her eyes welled up. "Of course."

I went back up to the ICU. Addison and I were there for another forty-five minutes before Doctor Berg walked back in. She checked the readings on the machine that monitored Collin's pulse and heart rate, then approached us. "Mrs. Park, I have some remarkable news."

"What?"

"I've never seen this before. Your son has been reinstated to the list. He'll receive the next compatible donor heart."

Addison stared at her in disbelief. "How did this happen?"

"That's above my pay grade. I don't know the whys, but our chief of staff signed off on the paperwork."

"Why would he do that?"

"I guess someone up there likes you."

"What's his name?" I asked. "Your chief of staff."

"Dr. Lawrence Pyranovich."

I glanced at Addison.

"Tell Doctor Pyranovich thank you," Addison said.

"Of course, we still have to wait for a compatible heart."

"How long can Collin last?"

"These kids are amazingly resilient; they can function at levels that would kill adults. I've seen children in his condition last for more than a week. I think he has a good chance."

After the doctor left, Addison fell into me and cried. "There's a chance."

I couldn't share her joy. She looked up at me. "What's wrong, why aren't you happy?"

"I have to tell you something. But I don't want to."

Her eyes showed her fear. "What?"

"The day we left your home, Collin told me . . ." I hesitated. "He told me he would die before Christmas."

She stared at me. "Why would he say that?"

"He said your father came to him and told him."

She lifted her hand to her eyes and began to cry.

"I'm sorry I didn't tell you sooner. Collin made me promise not to tell you."

Addison began to sob. When she had gained enough composure to speak, she said, "I knew. I already knew. I just didn't want to believe it." She looked into my eyes. "But I need to hear it from him."

The nurses checked Collin's vital signs every ten minutes through the night. At around two thirty A.M. a nurse removed the oxygen mask, replacing it with a double-pronged nasal tube. It was around four in the morning when Collin woke. Addison had fallen asleep, and I gently shook her. She looked up at me. "He's awake," I whispered.

She went to the side of his bed. Mother and son looked into each others eyes. "Hey, little man."

Collin didn't speak. After ten minutes, he closed his eyes again. I pushed a chair over next to the bed, and Addison sat and looked at him. Twenty minutes later his eyes opened again. This time she stood, clutching his hand. "Collin, I need to ask you something."

He stared at her.

"Can you hear me?"

He slowly nodded.

Addison swallowed. "Are you supposed to die?"

He blinked several times. Then he nodded. Addison's eyes closed and she took a deep breath. "Are you sure?"

He nodded.

"Do you want to go to *the other place*?"

His eyes filled with tears. He shook his head.

"Oh, baby." She stroked his cheek.

I bowed my head.

"Okay." Addison squared her shoulders and turned to me. "Tell Dr. Berg I'll sign the DNR."

"Should I get Elizabeth?"

She nodded. I found Dr. Berg and told her; she didn't understand Addison's change of heart. Then I went back down to the waiting room. Elizabeth was stretched across a row of seats, her head still in Miche's lap. Miche leaned sideways, asleep. I gently woke her. "I need Elizabeth now."

"Is it time?"

"I don't know."

I took Elizabeth in my arms; she woke in the elevator. "Can Collin come home now?"

I couldn't answer. I set Elizabeth down at the entrance to the ICU, and we walked to Collin's bed. Addison turned to us. "Come here, Lizzy."

Elizabeth knew more than we thought she did. She went up to the side of the bed and reached through the bars to touch her brother. "Hi, Collin."

He looked at her. They didn't speak. "I love you," she said. She leaned her head against the bars.

I put my hand on Addison's shoulder. "Did Doctor Berg come in?"

She nodded.

There was nothing left to do now but wait.

✦

About twenty minutes later, a dark-haired young doctor in a rumpled white coat walked into Collin's room. He crouched down next to Addison. "Mrs. Park? There's a woman in the room next to your son's. She and her husband were in a car accident. Her husband was DOA, and she's bleeding internally; we can't stop the hemorrhaging. She's going to leave behind four children."

Addison looked at him sadly. "Why are you telling me this?"

"I know who your son is."

Addison looked down for a moment, then she looked up at her children. "Come here, Lizzy," she said. Elizabeth walked back to her mother. Addison said to me, "Will you hold her?" I lifted Elizabeth onto my lap. Addison stood and went to Collin's side. "Collin, do you know what this doctor wants?"

He nodded.

Her eyes again filled with tears. "I will do whatever you want me to do."

Collin stared intensely at her. I didn't hear or see him speak, but after a moment I saw Addison take a deep breath. "Okay, baby." Addison turned to the doctor. "Can you bring her in here?"

"Yes." The doctor left the room and returned a moment later with a nurse who pushed a gurney. The young woman on it was unconscious, and her skin was white, almost like wax. They rolled the gurney up against the side of Collin's bed. "Tell me what to do," the doctor said to Addison.

"He just needs to touch her."

Addison went to the other side of the bed. The doctor dropped the side rail of the woman's gurney, and then Collin's. He took her hand and placed it under Collin's. Collin's eyes closed. For a moment, nothing happened. Suddenly the woman began to shake violently enough to rattle the gurney.

The nurse crossed herself. The dying woman's eyes

opened, and she let out a loud groan. She looked up toward the ceiling, then she turned to look at Collin. "It's you."

Collin's eyes were closed, and his breathing grew labored.

"This boy, he . . ." She looked at him, struggling for breath. "You can't save yourself, can you?" She turned to Addison. "Are you his mother?"

Addison couldn't speak, but her tears were answer enough.

"I saw him. From above this room. He was glorious. The light around him was glorious." Her eyes filled. She looked around the room. "None of you could see it, could you?" She looked back into Addison's eyes. "I'm sorry. I know what he did. I'm so sorry."

"It was already too late for us," Addison said.

It wasn't a minute before the machines around Collin's bed began beeping wildly. Suddenly Collin looked up to the corner of the room. His lips moved. Addison leaned over the bed. "Is Grandpa here?" She looked to where Collin's eyes were set and she knew. "Please, Dad . . . don't take him." Then she looked back at her child, her gaze caressing the gentle contours of his face, grasping for one last image that could last the rest of her life. Then she lay her cheek against his and whispered, "Thank you for letting me be your mother. I love you. I always will." Then she looked back to the corner of the room. "Take care of my little boy."

✦

Nothing else was said. Somewhere, in the love and sorrow of the moment Collin quietly left us behind.

We buried Collin the day after Christmas. There were no reporters—no cameras or crowds. There were just a few of us gathered around the little casket.

It's been four years since that Christmas season. A thousand new sunrises. And with each new day, the world is a little different.

Addison and I got married the next spring. She is my home and my breath. Though we have grieved much over our loss, it has drawn our family closer, and each year has brought us to a new level of acceptance and maybe even understanding.

✦

I returned to MusicWorld on January seventh as the new head of security. Even though Miche and Martsie kept their word, some of the other ladies in the office weren't as forgiving. A week before Christmas, Stayner was suspended, then later dismissed. Shortly thereafter his wife dismissed him as well.

Epilogue

Now that I don't have to travel anymore, I've become a homebody. I even have a garden. I finally decided that Earl wasn't going anywhere so I bought him a new bowl. He died the next week.

I have a new assistant at work. As it turned out, Miche left me. She quit to have her baby—a healthy little boy she named Collin. As Collin once said, he couldn't help but heal those he loved. Miche brings her little boy around every week or so for Addison and me to watch. In a few more years, Elizabeth will be old enough to babysit. Life comes full circle.

Not surprisingly, Steve lost his job at the law firm. He moved east, though I think *fled* would be a more appropriate word. He's now an ambulance chaser, with his smiling face on billboards promising wealth for pain. He still hasn't taken Elizabeth to Disneyland.

A few weeks into the New Year, I came across Riley Franzen's obituary on the business page of the *Tribune*. So it goes.

I visit my mother every month now. I wish I could tell you there had been some miraculous healing that cured her dementia and brought her back. But life's not really like that, at least not without Collin. But my heart is different toward her. And that's more than I could have hoped for.

I've pondered the events of that Christmas season many times over the last four years, and I've come to this conclusion: Throughout history there have been extraordinary people who don't seem to belong to this earth. People like Gandhi, Socrates, and Jesus. The world never knows what to do with these souls. Usually, we kill them. Then, years or centuries after they're gone, we embrace them and we begin to learn. We're peculiar beings. We stone our prophets, then build monuments to them after they're gone.

I believe Collin was one of those souls. And if he never had the global impact of a Gandhi, it doesn't matter. He changed our world.

There was so much we could have learned from Collin, about the next world or even the potential of this one. In some ways Collin became the canvas on which we painted our souls: in brilliance or darkness, the colors pulled from the palette of our desires. I've come to know that what we want in life is the greatest indication of who we really are.

We all have need of healing. And while our world spends billions of dollars each year on pills, potions, and procedures, it is all a shadow of what we need most. What good is a life prolonged if it only extends the season of cowardice and sin? What good is a new heart if it's only to be filled with hate or regret—or new eyes, if all they can see is criticism and intolerance? These are questions we must all ask ourselves. Perhaps the artificial heart is the perfect metaphor of our age.

I believe that what was most remarkable about Collin was not his gift but, rather, his choice to use it. Collin healed me. Not just my bronchitis or even my Tourette's, but in ways much more profound. For the best of all physical healing is just a delay of the inevitable. We all arrived on earth with a round-trip ticket, and someday we will all go to the *other place.* What Collin gave me was forever. He gave me back my soul.

Life goes on. Addison and I deal with life one day at a time as we raise our little girl. Elizabeth is now nine, the same age Collin was when he left us. Collin's death left a hole in many hearts, but perhaps hers most of all. He was her best friend, her hero, and her brother. Her rambunctiousness is gone, as is her frivolity. It was more than six months before I heard her laugh again. Today she is a thoughtful, tender little girl.

In the beginning, I said this wasn't a Christmas story. I may be wrong. One night, about six months ago, as I tucked Elizabeth into bed, she told me that Collin had come to her in a dream. "Don't cry so much," he said. "In the end, love wins."

There could be no greater message of Christmas than that.

hen Richard Paul Evans sat down to write *The Christmas Box*, he never imagined his book would become a #1 bestseller. The quiet story of parental love and the true meaning of Christmas made history when it became simultaneously the #1 hardcover and paperback book in the nation. Since then, he has since written eleven consecutive *New York Times* bestsellers. He is one of the few authors in history to have hit both the fiction and nonfiction bestseller lists and has won several awards for his books, including the 1998 American Mothers Book Award, two first place Storytelling World Awards, and the 2005 Romantic Times Best Women Novel of the Year Award.

Four of Evans' books have been made into major television productions, starring such acclaimed actors as Maureen O'Hara, James Earl Jones, Richard Thomas, Ellen Burstyn, Naomi Watts, Vanessa Redgrave, Christopher Lloyd, and Rob Lowe.

During the spring of 1997, Evans founded The Christmas Box House International, an organization devoted to building shelters and providing services for abused and neglected children. Such shelters are operational in Moab, Vernal, Ogden, and Salt Lake City, Utah. To date more than 13,000 children have been housed in Christmas Box House facilities. In addition, his book *The Sunflower* was the motivating factor in the creation of The Sunflower Orphanage in Peru. Evans was awarded the Volunteers of America National Empathy Award and the Washington Times Humanitarian of the Century Award. Evans is also the founder and CEO of BookWise, an international direct sales business.

As an acclaimed speaker, Evans has shared the podium with such notable personalities as President George W. Bush, President George and Barbara Bush, former British Prime Minister John Major, Ron Howard, Elizabeth Dole, Deepak Chopra, Steve Allen, and Bob Hope. Evans has been featured on *The Today Show* and *Entertainment Tonight*, as well as in *Time, Newsweek, People, The New York Times, Washington Post, Good Housekeeping, USA Today, TV Guide, Reader's Digest,* and *Family Circle.* Evans lives in Salt Lake City, Utah, with his wife, Keri, and their five children.

Join Richard's mailing list and receive free reading group discussion guides, book and tour updates, special sneak previews of upcoming projects, and other special offers available only for his mailing list.

To join, visit Richard's Web site now at:
www.richardpaulevans.com